First edition August 2021

www.talesbybob.com

Introduction

Howard Marsh is a lot of things: a liar, a thief, a poor man's wizard. He's a shoddily tattooed skin stretched over a too skinny body that's barely held together by the same drugs that are tearing his life apart. A cynic, his words are often as poison as the substances he takes to pass his days, a suicide attempt years in the making.

He's the scion of a family with a history as rich as it is materially poor. He's the product of a miserable county with more dirt roads than paved, where poverty and loss is the order of the day. He's a man haunted by his past, and has yet to find any reason to try and piece himself back together.

You would be well advised to take what he says with a large grain of salt. He will cover the worst parts, glossing over the bits that show his darkest sides. The bits where the drugs that ravage him are in control. Where we find him is at the bottom, eking out a living as a water witch, a copper thief, a finder of lost things. Living in a storage shed and trying to maintain what's left of his frayed relationships with the few family members who will still talk to him.

But dear readers, he's a better man than he thinks. He doesn't see it; he's long forgotten the possibility even, and no one left in his life sees it either. But, if you can endure the miserable existence of watching someone make nothing but bad choices for a time, then you will perhaps be rewarded. Maybe you will see him slowly scrabble out of the muddy, trash filled ditch that is his life.

It won't be quick, and it won't be painless. The stories to come are often filled with sadness. The fairytale ending is not for stories such as these. There is a chance at happiness, but it is a long way away, and there are many obstacles both in him, and in his path.

This is not a plea for understanding, or forgiveness, or any sort of justification. It is just the way of things.

He is Howard Marsh, the Methgician.

And he doesn't give a damn what you think.

Bringing Home The Rain

Being the first tale in the Redemption of Howard Marsh.

1. A Conversation At The U-Store-It (Fall)

With a groan, I rolled up the door to my storage unit and stepped outside. The mid-morning sun was blinding compared to the utter darkness inside my unit, so I shaded my eyes with one hand and stretched deeply. A yawn forced its way past my stiffened jaw, causing it to pop painfully, and was escorted by a sound echoing in my back.

I didn't remember much from last night, but as I rubbed my tender jaw, a brief memory of a fist colliding with my face bubbled up. I decided not to think too hard on it; I had probably deserved it, and ignorance is frequently bliss. I am a snarky shit sometimes - one of my many fine qualities that have so endeared me to my local community.

The fall air was cool enough that I wished I had taken time to put on some clothes instead of stepping out in just my faded blue boxers, but I decided it was too late now. I knew I made quite a sight: a short, wiry man with disheveled black hair and a few days worth of stubble across my chin that danced along that fine line between rugged and rough-looking. A battered pair of glasses sat across the bridge of my oft broken nose, held together with a little bit of electrical tape. When I smiled, you'd notice more than a few missing teeth, but then I had the sort of pale blue eyes that women seemed to like. A pair of untied combat boots loosely encasing my feet completed the look, a fitting match for the plethora of poorly done tattoos that dotted my body. I was a hot mess, but I had long embraced that fact.

Gravel crunching underfoot, I made my way down the row of storage units. Built from cinder blocks and tin, they'd been painted white once, though most had flaked back to their natural gray. They'd been my home for years now, long enough that I knew each faded red roll-up door like an old friend. I could even pretty well tell you what each one held, having spent time rummaging through them each, in turn, late at night when the only security light flickered off.

Rounding the corner, I leaned against the wall and groaned. My whole body ached; that sort of deep pain you get from drinking too hard and falling asleep on a concrete floor. Without leaning up, I relieved myself against the fence that separated the Elk Grove U-Store-It from the backlot of the Dairy Queen.

Through the cracks in the wooden fence, I could see the back of the rusted green dumpster with its accompanying grease trap. Even if I hadn't seen it, I could easily have smelled it, the reek of rancid food filling my nostrils. Beyond that, a small line of cars filled the drive-through of the restaurant, which immediately told me it had to be at least ten in the morning. Over the sounds of engine noise, I could hear something rustling in the dumpster, though whether it was a cat or possum was anyone's guess.

Tucking myself away, I came back around the corner just in time to see my only neighbor, Corey Davis, sliding up the rolling door to his unit. What was meant to be an overnight stay three years ago when his wife kicked him out had become a more permanent situation, but I certainly did not begrudge him a stay in my little slice of paradise.

He nodded to me as I passed. Corey was not a morning person, and he looked about as rough as I did, wearing a pair of plaid pajama bottoms coupled with a sweat-stained wife beater. He had to walk carefully so as not to knock over the numerous empty beer bottles that littered his floor, and judging from his bloodshot eyes, most of those were from the night before. Had we been drinking? Had he been the one who hit me? Wouldn't be the first time.

I knew I wouldn't get a word out of him for at least a half hour even if I wanted to, so I just returned the nod and dipped back into Casa del Marsh. Pulling the chain, the yellow bulb that was the room's only source of light flickered on fitfully, but coupled with the morning sun, it gave me enough illumination to try and find some clothes. I rummaged around until I found a pair of cutoff jean shorts, which I paired with an Atlanta Braves shirt I'd taken from a box someone had left behind the Christian Mission. I didn't give a rip about sports typically, but it was a damn nice shirt, and as shitty as I felt, I decided that maybe I would attempt to spend the day faking it till I made it. Look good, feel good.

Dressed, I wandered to the back of my shed where I kept my food. I reached inside my mini-fridge to grab a beer, and cracking it open, I slumped into the worn recliner that doubled as my bed. I figured a little hair of the dog that bit me would have me feeling better soon enough. Then I might dive into a honeybun, or maybe some Spam.

In a moment or two, I would start in on one of my other bad habits, but the beer would do until I could fully wake up. I thought about going back to sleep but decided against it...these drugs weren't going to do themselves. If it hadn't been a weekday, Corey might have joined me, but seeing as he actually had a job, as an accountant of all things, I knew he wouldn't.

I was reaching under my chair for my little box of oblivion when I heard the sound of tires rolling over the gravel. Swearing, I sat up straight, leaving the box in place for now. It was probably just someone coming to see Corey, some poor sod who could only afford an accountant that had his office in a storage shed, but it paid to be at least somewhat cautious, I figured.

A heartbeat later, I watched as a jet black Suburban pulled up about ten feet from my door and came to a halt. The doors opened and a trio of men stepped out wearing dark-colored suits. One of those suits contained a man I knew, and I grimaced.

"Mr. Marsh, pleasure to see you once more," said the grey haired man striding towards me. The other two men, aviator glasses mirroring the area, hung back, leaning against the SUV. I could see the telltale hint of a bulge that had to be pistol holsters on their side.

"Agent Rutherford. Wish I could say the same."

The agent belonged to some alphabet agency that I struggled to recall. NOAA? That seemed right, but fuck, who can keep them all straight. We'd had a few run-ins over the years, ones that rarely ended very favorably for me. He knew what I could do, and was not above using me for his own ends. And I suspected, using me up, if needed. Slipping off his sunglasses, he slid them into his breast pocket and stepped inside.

His face twitched almost imperceptibly as the disarray of my living quarters hit him. "Quite the tidy little domicile you have here, Marsh. About what I expected if I'm being honest." His nose scrunched. "When was the last time you bathed, man? Jesus."

I ran my fingers through my greasy hair on purpose and smiled sourly. "A week or so, I guess. If'n you'd called, I would have picked up for you. Taken a bath in the Jacuzzi tub I keep in the guest house maybe."

Rutherford ignored my snark. "We may have another incident on our hands, and I want you to look into it."

I took a sip of my beer, a trickle of the cool liquid escaping my lips to dribble down my chin. "Not interested."

Rutherford grinned. It was a predatory thing, all teeth and meanness. Reminded me of my daddy's when he had a good drunk going. "I don't particularly care. Your state of desire doesn't frequently figure into my calculations."

I just gave him a blank stare that I hoped conveyed my extreme disinterest. It lost some effect in that he wasn't even looking at me, but was instead leaning down to look at the little stack of books I had by the door.

"Ten miles south of here," he began, at last looking up from his perusal, "it hasn't rained in 7 months."

I was digging around the cracks of the recliner trying to find my lighter, but found time to scoff instead. "It stormed here last week. Blew down a tree, near about took out the police station. Didn't, mores the pity, but it is what it is."

Rutherford nodded. "I'm well aware. In fact, in the past seven months, there have been a number of storms that have hit Elk Grove, and Jubal County in general. In that time, the weathermen tell me that every inch of the county has gotten at least several inches of rain. Except for a five mile circle just south of here. They say when you watch the radar, the clouds part right around it every time."

"Weather's funny like that," I opined. I had found my lighter and managed to match it to the nub of cigarette from my makeshift ashtray.

"Marsh, I am going to level with you. We don't know what's going on. We suspect it's something in your realm. So get to it. Solve the problem, before more folks start to notice. We will pay the standard rate, as always."

I took a deep drag, deep enough that it killed the little bit of tobacco, and then chased it with a sip of beer. "Rutherford?"

He arched an eye.

"Fuck off."

Rutherford grinned that vicious smile again. Reaching into his breast pocket, he pulled out his glasses and slipped them onto his face. He nodded to one of his men, who pulled out a phone. Something was up, I could tell. The bastard had an ace up his sleeve, else he wouldn't have bothered coming out here.

The agent pulled a business card out and set it on the arm of my recliner, careful not to touch me as he did so. "My number is on there. If I might make a suggestion, perhaps you should remember it. You know, for your one phone call."

My stomach knotted as I heard sirens turn on. Nearby. Way too nearby. I jumped to my feet. "The fuck did you do?"

Rutherford stepped back out into the light. "I guess that gentleman you 'assaulted' last night pressed charges. What a shame." He opened his door, and one foot inside turned to face me. "Be a peach and give us a ring if you change your mind."

I stepped out, ready to run, but before I could even get good and started, the cops were wheeling into the lot, lights flashing. Swearing, I flipped off Rutherford's SUV as it pulled away, and stepped back inside. I killed my beer and then scooped up the man's card, muttering a small Word and flicking my wrist just so it made a slight...crinkle...in reality, causing the card to vanish. I made sure my stash of drugs were well hidden, as best as I could in the time I had.

The cops rolled to a stop, and I made my way outside with my hands up. I knew the drill all too well. Corey had stepped out too, shading his eyes against the sun. "Be seeing you, Marsh?"

I nodded. This wasn't the first time he had witnessed me get hauled off, and I strongly suspected it would not be the last. "Thanks man. Lock up for me?"

He said he would, and went back into his unit. Then the cops had me on the ground. Same shit, different day.

2. A Field Trip To The City Jail

If the cops were a little rough with me, well, I would be the first to admit it wasn't entirely undeserved. I had gotten on a first name basis with pretty much all of them, both city cops and county sheriffs, all of them for the wrong reasons. In some of my "higher moments," I had perhaps given one or more the odd bite or black eye. So I couldn't rightly fault them for erring on the side of caution, even if I was pretty sure I would be picking gravel out of my knees for the rest of the day.

It was a dismal ride to the station in a cop car that reeked of cleaning supplies. They must have busted a drunk last night, and the poor soul had hurled all over the backseat. That was most likely an added factor to the surly attitudes of the men in blue in front of me, who had shut down my every attempt at civil conversation. I just shrugged and went back to staring out the window.

Elk Grove was a miserable place, but it was my home. It had just enough for a man to survive, but a man sometimes wants to do more than just survive. Luckily, Montgomery was only 40 minutes away, and that was a place you could do a little living if you knew the right people. And like all good rural areas, the drugs were plentiful enough. They certainly helped relieve the monotony of daily life.

We passed through a town that could go from movie set idealism to the dungy truth of southern life in a matter of houses. You'd have some old folks' white-painted home with a too-nice yard sitting next to a place that had enough scrap metal lying about the yard to keep me in rent for a month of Sundays. The only business we passed that seemed to be really popping was the Piggly Wiggly, although there were more than a few cars parked in front of the ABC store, waiting for it to open at eleven no doubt.

Elk Grove was small enough to not have been rightly killed by a Walmart yet, so the square around the courthouse was still mostly full of stores. The Court Square Cafe, Jones Hardware, Jernigan Hunting Supplies, Quick Cuts, and the usual cross section of what a city needed when they were too lazy to drive some place with better prices. In the middle of it all squatted the Courthouse, the tallest building in the county with its clock tower that chimed every day at noon.

The jail was a small building set off behind the courthouse, surrounded by a number of old oak trees so the eyes of the city would not be affronted by the sights of lowly criminals such as ourselves. Sun-bleached bricks with grey barred windows, I suppose I can understand where the city was coming from. It was not a stately edifice by any stretch.

A few shoves, a few curses (going both ways, mind you), and I was safely ensconced in my home away from home once more, dressed in an ill-fitting orange jumpsuit. I wished I could remember the details from last night, but I was sure one side of it would come out soon enough. If I let it get that far.

I muttered that small Word again and snapped. Rutherford's card appeared in between my fingers. I eyed it a bit, and began slowly twirling it as I weighed my options.

On the one hand, the city jail was not that bad. A few days' stay and I would likely be out again. When you are as annoying as myself, they tend to do what they can to be rid of you as quickly as possible. I would have some community service to try and weasel out of, some more time tacked onto my court referral program, and of course new rounds of fines. The county just couldn't do without a little bit of financial serfdom from one of its favorites.

On the downside, it was sometimes hard to get my chosen forms of entertainment. Just depended on who decided to get caught during my stay. Or who worked their shift at the jail. There was already a crawling itch creeping up my spine informing me that there was a solid desire for illicit substances to enter my body. Sooner rather than later.

Rutherford could save me all that hassle. But then I would have to do what he asked. And I, without fail, regretted getting involved in his bullshit. Moreover, it was not like doing the job would get me in his good graces. I was convinced no such thing existed.

He did pay though. I was about a month behind on the rent on my unit, as I hadn't had as much luck scrounging up copper of late as I usually did, and scrap metal prices had bottomed out. I'd made a touch cleaning up some limbs in last week's storm from some of the houses near the storage unit, but that money had been magically transformed into a Dairy Queen ice cream cake during a late night smoke session.

Homelessness was not the optimal choice.

I lay there on my cot, weighing my options. A groan from the next cell roused me from my introspection. A bulbous man was lying on the adjacent cot, so soused with alcohol that I could smell him sweating it out. You likely could have gotten drunk just by taking a lick of that man's forehead. And then he puked. The smell that came with it implied that he had gotten so drunk as to eat something decaying.

I rose to my feet. "Guard! Lemme get that phone call now, please!"

3. A Marsh On The Town

Six hours after that first trip outside my storage unit, I stepped back out into the light of day for the second time. It galled me to have to call Rutherford, but the man had been good as his word. Within a few minutes of my call, the cops started the release process.

Rutherford himself was not there to greet me as I exited. In truth, I had been a little surprised to see him make the trip out at all; usually, he either had me brought to him or sent an underling. My guess was that he suspected I would say no, and got sick satisfaction of personally getting me sent to jail. He was that sort of ass.

So while there was no devil in a suit himself, there was a minion of his in a black SUV. Wearing a suit identical to those I had seen Rutherford's men wearing earlier, it could have been one of the ones from before, but I couldn't tell. They all appeared identical to me.

"Howard Marsh?"

He must not have been then. I barely resisted the urge to get snarky, and instead just nodded.

"Here." He handed me a thin folder. A quick glance revealed a couple of maps and some assorted papers. I would look later.

I tucked the folder under my arm. "And my cash?"

The man pulled a plain white envelope from his jacket. "200 in tens, as requested. A further 800, plus expenses upon completion."

The usual deal, one I could certainly live with. That 200 was over 3 months' rent. Not that it would go to that most likely. Rent could come later and it usually did. "Yeah, yeah, I know the deal. But I hafta have receipts for it to count as an expense. And drugs are not a valid expense, says your accountants."

The agent's lip curled a little. "Correct. Now, I am authorized to take you someplace within a few miles of here, then I have to go back to the field office. Where would you like to go?"

A free ride...that was new. I figured that was Rutherford's mea culpa for having me locked up. My first thought was a quick trip over to Jimmy's, but I suspected taking some sort of federal agent to my drug dealer's would not go over well. Seeing Jimmy go diving out the back of his camper could almost be worth it though...

"I got a place. Hop in, I'll tell you how to get there."

Other than cop cars, I did not often get to ride in a nice vehicle. The ones I found myself in had peeling interiors, missing headlights, non-functioning air conditioners, or all of the above. So it was a pleasant change to find myself in the front seat of a posh SUV with all the bells and whistles. Clearly whatever agency they worked for had not suffered the same declining fortunes that Jubal County had over the past eight years.

I looked over at the agent as he started down the drive from the jail. "You're gonna swing me by my shed, then take me to my destination. Copacetic?"

I think he glowered at me, but from behind those cliché sunglasses, I couldn't rightly tell. His tone helped my deduction however. "I am taking you one place. Not two."

"Right. Swinging me by my shed on the way to Lidda's."

"Pick one. The shed or Lidda's. Not both. I have things to do."

I grinned over at the man as I produced a cigarette from behind my ear. "You know where Lidda's is?"

He gave a curt shake of his head.

"Well to get there, what do ya know, you gotta go by my shed."

Staring ahead at the road, he deadpanned. "I guess I'm just dropping you off at your shed then."

I lit the cigarette and rolled the window down a crack. Before the first wisp of smoke could even reach the vented airway the agent was snaking his hand out to try and grab my smoke. "You can't smoke in here!"

I easily dodged his grasping hand. "And yet I am. Funny how that works. What's also gonna be funny is what happens if you just leave me at my shed, with no way to get to Lidda's."

The agent's jaw worked soundlessly for a moment, and then subsided, and I knew that I had won. That's the thing about me, as most folks come to learn. Most times, it's easier to let me have my way. Save your time and energy fussing, do what I ask, and it'll all work out for the best.

For me at least. Depending on your definition of "best."

We rode in silence to my shed. Corey had closed up his home shed and opened up his work shed with its tiny sign that said "Davis Accounting" swinging idly in the breeze. Judging from the ratty mustang convertible out front, he had a client in there, so I decided against bugging him. Plus I didn't want to test the agent's patience too far.

Opening up my shed, I beelined for my chair and quickly dug out my black box of oblivion. Just holding it calmed the itch that was filling me up and threatening to make me crazy. Box in hand, I scooped up a honey bun from my food shelf, and with another half pack of cigarettes tucked in my back pocket, bopped my way back to the SUV.

Clambering back inside, I smiled. "To Lidda's Jeeves, and don't spare the horses!"

I gave him the directions, then set about sorting through my box. When the agent saw my pawing through my drugs, he had the good sense to stay quiet, but I could see his hands tighten on the wheel. I was getting a little short on needles, but I could remedy that easily enough. Out of courtesy, I decided to hold off until I reached Lidda's. It was the least I could do, I supposed.

To pass the time, I pointed out some of the more interesting sights of the area. As we exited the nearer environs of Elk Grove, I pointed to a burned-out church. The

Church of Signs Revealed had never been very large, but it had been pretty in a small, quaint way. The Spanish moss hanging from the surrounding trees, caught in a breeze like it was, seemed almost to be reaching for the charred husk. It was an eerily beautiful sight. "That's the church they say Thomas Richmond burned down."

"The church he *did* burn down," corrected the agent.

I snorted. "I shared a glass pipe or two with Tom over the years. The boy ain't no arsonist. I don't care what the news reports say."

I had never gotten all the details, but I knew there was more to the tale. The Richmond family was old around these parts, and stories had all sorts of strange occurrences tied to the line. They were kin to the Marshes - if not in blood, then in spirit.

The agent started prattling on about how Thomas was caught red-handed and whatnot. I just decided to keep my mouth shut and ignore him. Being caught doing a thing was not a good enough reason. I'd been caught doing things I had never done, or done for reasons anyone who wasn't in my shoes would ever understand.

Something about seeing that church caused my good mood to vanish. Even my brief stint in jail, coupled with Rutherford's bullshit had not managed to get me down. But seeing those charred white boards...I felt like a balloon someone had let all the air out of. I just gazed out the window, not seeing anything but the faint ghost of my reflection on the glass, and once, a purple car sitting out in a field.

By the time we reached Lidda's, he had given up trying to convince me. As he slid into the rutted drive, I muttered a vague thanks I didn't really feel, and made sure I had gathered up my things. With one final check, I stepped out into the yard, and gave a listless wave to the man to let him know I was clear.

4. Lidda's

The yard was scattered with toys, most of them broken or covered in a layer of dirt and dust. The first falling leaves of the season were beginning to cluster around the edges of the yard, drifting in the afternoon breeze. There was the occasional sprout of grass struggling to grow up from the clay soil, but they were the exception. Rutted, eroded red clay was the order of the day - the sort that was occasionally filled in with sand, or road dirt, only to be washed away with the next long rain.

On the edge of the woods, a rusted-out Camaro slowly decayed to a shell of what it had been. Its dry rotted tires were flat on the ground, and its windshield had been shattered, no doubt by one of Lidda's spawn. When we'd both been younger, we'd ridden many a mile in that car, but then the transmission had worn out, and it'd been dumped there to die.

Lidda's trailer had seen better days. This was the case with most of Jubal County of course, but with her trailer you had the sense that its better days were perhaps a few years farther back than most. It was fortunate in that it was brown, so the rust patches blended in almost, but that did little to hide the sheer number of dents in its thin tin sides. It looked as though some giant had left it in its pocket with the loose change too long.

The squawking of an infant was piercing out from within it somewhere and I cringed. I had forgotten about the latest little fuck trophy. With a sigh, I made my way across the toy and trash strewn yard and towards the rickety steps that would take me inside.

Lidda was an ex-girlfriend, one of three that would at least still give me the benefit of talking first before shooting. If I had been the type to have had a high school sweetheart, she might have even qualified. Of course we had both dropped out at the beginning of tenth grade, so maybe we didn't quite fit the bill. I went on and got my GED. She went on and got pregnant. With some other dude's kid.

That was the end of that.

A mix of guilt and my dogged persistence had convinced her that it would just be easiest to let me hang around on occasion. Over the years, we had hooked up a few dozen times, amongst the revolving door of boyfriends and baby daddies. It had proven fairly lucrative for us both in fact: she living off the child support, me finding some of my better drug connections through her exes.

The main thing was she would let me come grab a shower any time I needed - which was rare, but after a stint in jail I always wanted to wash the cop off me. I didn't want to go into this job with the taint of a cell on me, which would most certainly be bad luck.

I decided not to knock, and just strode on in, stepping into a dingy living room with the only light coming from the late afternoon sunlight filtering through threadbare curtains that might have once been white. Whenever this little tin slice of paradise had been built, it was pretty clear that brown was the order of the day, which was for the best, as it did a halfway decent job of hiding decades of nicotine stains.

"Jesus Marsh, can't you knock?" shouted Lidda Smith/Richmond/Stuart ne' Hubbard. She had a red-faced kid tucked in one arm, a Virginia Slim clasped between her fingers, and a distinctive lack of pants coupled with a too-thin wife beater and no bra. The room was fairly sweltering, so I didn't blame her for her lack of clothing. And had I been in a better mood, I might have taken a bit longer in staring, especially as she made no move to cover herself. But I just didn't have it in me. I needed a shower.

Besides, it was certainly nothing I hadn't seen before, and obviously seen in better days. Her blonde hair was pulled back in a loose ponytail, stray hairs framing her tired brown eyes. Her skin was tan, though the wife beater revealed stark lines of white where her swimsuit had covered her as she'd lay down out in the backyard that summer.

With my eyes closed, I could have picked out and drawn you each of the tattoos she had. The magnolia on her thigh she'd gotten for her granny when she'd died. The names of her kids on her arms. The angel wings she had on one shoulder that she'd gotten after she miscarried. The roses she'd gotten to try and cover her c-section scars.

"Power shut off again?" I called over my shoulder as I started down the dark, narrow hallway to her bedroom. I knew the answer, but I figured I would ask anyway.

A creeping note of shame entered her voice. "Just till Earl's check clears. He said I could cash it tomorrow, just gotta make it till then."

The rest of her kids were gone, it seemed. She had four others, by three different husbands, but she managed to arrange it that their custody weekends all fell at the same time. Had it not been for her latest trip down maternity lane, she would actually have been able to have a weekend or two off from kids.

She followed me down the hall. She was saying something, but with my shirt over my head, I missed most of it, and ignored the rest. My pants and boxers followed a second later. "I take it Jimmy's at work?" Jimmy, the father of the child doing an admirable impersonation of a siren, was the latest beau. He worked for the county water company, and as far as her men went, he was by a landslide the pick of the litter.

"Yeah. For about another hour. He ain't living here right now, but he comes by after work to see the kid for a bit before going to his mama's." She paused. "We uh, we're working through some things right now."

Jimmy wasn't fond of me, surprisingly enough. So I decided I had a firm deadline of an hour. The shower would take five minutes, leaving me with a bit of time on my hands. I paused, and looked Lidda over once more, as I turned on the shower. Thin, too thin, but that was the drugs. And who was I to judge.

"Did Jimmy catch you with Keith again?" I asked while sticking my hand in the water, testing how warm it was.

She nodded sheepishly. I had a suspicion that pretty soon Jimmy would soon be just another check and Keith would be the next sucker. He'd come at a better time than most: she'd gotten her works tied up after the last one. Long time coming, if you asked me, but then folks typically didn't.

I watched as she bent over to pick up the kid's pacifier that it had dropped in its fit. "Well, how about you find a place to stow that kid and come join me?"

She eyed me warily. "You just got outta jail, right?"

"I'm here getting a shower, ain't I?"

She nodded. "What for?"

I stopped and thought for a moment. "You know, I still don't rightly know. Some Rutherford bullshit."

She knew about the agent. She gave a gentle shrug, and carefully put out her half-smoked cig in an overflowing ashtray by the bed, clearly intending to save it for later. "Lemme put him in his playpen."

I sat down on the toilet and opened my box of oblivion while I waited for the water to get warmer. That was the other reason why I opted to shower here: the power was off about as much as it was on, but the water heater was gas. It just took a long time to warm up.

By the time I had gotten the glass pipe lit and taken that first toe-curling, wind-blasting hit, she had gotten the kid down. It was still squawking, but quieter, and it was at least doing it off in the living room. I looked up to see her walking back in the room, pulling her shirt off and throwing it on the edge of the bed. Stepping out of her panties, she leaned in the bathroom doorway. Her ribs jutted out farther than her chest almost. Too skinny.

Well, any port in a storm.

"Lemme get some of that," she said, reaching for the oblivion in my hand.

5. A Late Afternoon Stroll

The sound of a truck pulling into the yard caught me by surprise. Luckily, I was already putting on my shoes because Lidda and I had finished up our drugs/fun/shower about five minutes earlier. I had known I had to be cutting it pretty close, but this was closer than I had anticipated for sure.

"Shit!" Lidda swore as she hurriedly jumped from the bed and started tugging on her panties. She looked at me, her eyes wide. "What the hell, Marsh, you know where the window is, get moving!"

Rolling my eyes, I scooped up my things and eased them out the back bedroom window. This was not the first time we had perpetrated this particular little fire drill over the years, not by far. The thin metal of the frame was even slightly bent from my hands and feet pressing down on them as I scampered through. It made the window hard to close, which was why more often than not it sat open.

Leaning out, I glanced down to make sure there were no glass bottles or the like for me to land on. I had done that once, barefoot, when her second husband came home early one day. Had to run a quarter mile with blood squirting from my heel. I never intended to repeat that particular debacle.

I paused for a moment and contemplated dropping a twenty or two to help with the power. But I didn't, as it would have most likely just led to some weird questions. Besides, Lidda would probably have been pissed. She was a lot of things, but she weren't no hooker.

I hit the ground just in time to hear the front door open. Grinning, I gathered my odds and ends and began traipsing off into the woods. The other perk of Lidda's was that her property abutted my grandmother's. That was how we first came to know each other; in fact, we met playing in the woods when we were just little things. A few miles walk, and I would be back in business.

That interlude had worked wonders on my mood. That awful itch was gone, I had gotten a little, and I even had a shower. I felt as good as a man could, I reckoned. And even with a little bit of gravel dust on my shirt, it was still looking fine. Look good, feel good.

I was humming right along on a cocktail of illicit substances, which I will admit left me oscillating wildly between intensely focused and wildly scattered. I was full to the brim with energy, damn near skipping along, leaving my fingers all sorts of twitchy. If there had been some music, I suspect I'd have been dancing. Instead, I made due by humming and strutting along like the king rooster in the pen.

It was getting on towards evening time now, and I felt like I should have a bite to eat. I wasn't hungry, but I recalled I hadn't eaten today. I would need to remedy that at some point, maybe with the honeybun I had with me, but for now I just focused on making my way through the woods.

This was about as pristine an oak forest as you could find in the area; in fact, I only knew of one better, and that one folks knew better than to go to. Here though, it was all fine tall white oaks, with a smattering of other assorted trees. This late in the year, a goodly number of the leaves had died and were starting to fall off, leaving a large number of dead leaves to crunch and shuffle around my feet. It was a surprisingly soothing sound, one I didn't get to hear as much in town. With everything in my system flowing along, the sounds were richer, deeper.

As the breeze picked up a bit, I could hear the faint sounds of bamboo wood chimes clanking eerily off to my left. A tiny shudder passed through me, and I started veering more to my right. What they called the old witch hut was out that way, and I was not exactly too anxious to find myself near there after dark.

I passed near a briar patch, and I paused long enough to see if any of the blackberries were still edible this late in the year. I could see them there, what looked to be the dark ripeness I was hoping for, but I looked closer regardless. A handful of berries would do nothing for my hunger, not really, but I had a powerful love of the little things. And being free, that was my favorite flavor. I was out of luck, however, with every one I could find being a withered black berry, dried out and good for little more than some half-starved possum.

A good fifteen-minute walk had me leaving the forest and setting foot in the old cow pasture. There hadn't been a cow living there since my granddaddy had been alive, and the grass was near knee high, even that late in the year. I had to at least be a little careful, as there were all manner of little potholes scattered across the field, hidden by the grass, and more than once I'd twisted an ankle in one.

I could, for the first time, see my granny's house, as well as those of some of my uncles. All three homes were spread across about a mile of ridgeline on the far side of the pasture, and as it grew darker, I could see lights start to wink on inside. While the other two were small brick houses, Granny's was a sprawling two-story antebellum house that dominated the hilltop like some old castle. Its white paint was flaking, but at this distance, and in the rising dusk, it appeared almost spectral. Like some ancient ghost prowling the hilltop, looking for souls to steal.

My stomach gave a growl, though any feeling of hunger was still subdued. I suspected I would find some sort of tasty morsel to mangle with my teeth once I got to where I was headed. I decided to give Granny's a wide berth and head for Uncle Hubert Dale's, her youngest son, and the uncle I was closest to.

I was just entering the yard when he stepped out onto the narrow strip of porch that ran the width of his small house. "Bout time you showed. 'Spected you a good half hour ago," was what he said by way of greeting. I didn't bother to ask how he knew about my imminent arrival. In a family like mine, such things come to be expected.

His prematurely greying hair was shoulder length, and he was possessed of the same gaunt frame that the men of the Marsh clan were prone to. He had on an old pair of camouflage pants, pretty much the only kind of pants he ever wore, with some sort of free blood donation shirt. It hung loosely on him, being a size or two too large, but that was how he liked them. The porch light was behind him leaving his front mostly in shadow, but his scruffy face was lit by the red tip of his cigarette, and I could see he was grinning. "See you came cross the field. Been over at Lidda's?"

My boots clumped up the few steps. I winked. "Perhaps. Give me some of that pork steak I smell and maybe I'll tell you about it."

He laughed, a reedy sound that descended into a hacking cough. He waved me on in. "I knewed you was hungry."

He kept a tidy place - albeit a bit spare - just a few old and simple pieces of furniture paired with a couple of wedding pictures up on the wall. Uncle Hubert Dale was somewhat of a minimalist, with a place that could do with some cluttering up. It practically made my skin crawl, all those unused surfaces. Could pile a lot of scavenged treasure in a place like this.

There was a plate on the table with a fat, fried pork steak sitting on it, accompanied with a huge pile of roasted potatoes, all set out for me. I sidled up to the table and started to dig in. H.D. settled in across from me, opening a High Life as he did.

Taking a long drag on his smoke, he breathed out. "So what brings you out this way, boy? Besides my cooking, that is."

I didn't even slow down shoveling food into my mouth. It has been often said that table manners are not my strong suit. But then folks say a lot of things. Speaking from around a mouth full of food, I started to relate to him the course of the day's events. By the time I sopped up the last of the grease with a fork full of potatoes, I had him pretty well caught up. He had sat through the whole recitation in silence, and when he saw that I was done, he grabbed my plate and took it over to the sink and started to rinse it off.

Over the sound of the water, he asked, "How about you get that folder of stuff laid out, and we can take a look at it proper like, see if we can get a handle on it?"

It occurred to me that I hadn't bothered to give it a good going-over myself, which wasn't like me at all. Subconsciously, I supposed I *really* didn't want the job. The folder was sitting under my little box, so I pulled it out and laid out all the sheets side by side.

The first was a map of Jubal County. An area a bit east of Granny's, maybe ten miles or so, was encircled in a red swoop, but otherwise it was just a typical county survey map. The next was a close-up map of the area, with property lines and such. Other than that, the others were just weather reports. I didn't bother reading them, I would just take Rutherford's word for it and save myself some time. The maps were the key to this.

H.D. was standing over the table, his hands planted on its top as he stared at the maps. "Well then," was all he said.

I eyed him over. "Any more starting insights you'd like to posit there H.D.?"

He slowly shook his head. "Nope. Nothing sticking out at me. I mean, I know the area of course. But nothing too special about it. Right on the edge of Bay Houdan, but misses it a bit. Not sure if that matters. And it's not quite a perfect circle, a bit more oblong I suppose. But just a little."

I looked; he was correct in that. It wasn't so much that it really stood out at you, but with a little looking you could tell. "Know anyone over that way?"

He leaned back, and finding the chair with his legs, sat down. "Oh yeah. Quite a few, I suppose. My first wife's folks were from that area. Kershaws. Nice family for the most part, 'cept for one crazy daughter that I had the ill luck of marrying. Bunch of peanut farmers by and large."

I frowned. "When I asked, I sorta hoped you might know someone with their finger a little more on the pulse than a peanut farmer."

He arched an eye at me. "You think someone will have a better grasp on the weather than a farmer?"

"Touché." I produced a smoke and lit it up. Staring at the papers, I mulled things over. If folks knew what was going on, Rutherford's agents would likely have ferreted it out. So clearly, whatever was going on lay outside the sort of questions even well-grounded federal agents and your normal farmers and housewives would ask. Whatever it was, it lay down the path less taken.

I asked the question I didn't want to ask. "Should I talk to Granny?"

H.D. stiffened. "I would leave her out of things unless really needed. She's on more of a tear than usual. Best to stay clear."

I breathed a little sigh of relief. I had hoped he would say that. As little contact as possible with Granny almost always proved best.

Hubert Dale shook himself a little, clearly chasing out bad thoughts. Looking over at me, he paused thoughtfully, stroking his chin. His calloused fingers made a rasping noise as they passed over the stubble. "My thinking is that someone has put a curse out on someone. You find out who and why, problem solved."

It was the obvious solution. But finding that could be like looking for a needle in a haystack. I swore lightly under my breath. "I reckon you're right. Gonna need to borrow the van. Is that alright?"

He frowned at me. "Gonna put gas in it this time?"

6. A Solitary Ride

H.D. offered to ride with me, perhaps to make an introduction or two. But in the end, I left him behind. I was pretty sure his real motive was to keep an eye on me and make sure I didn't damage his van. But I wasn't sure what sort of timeline I was looking at with this job, and if he came along, sure as the world, we'd end up getting sidetracked with his bullshit along the way.

Unlike his house, my uncle kept his van in a suitable state of trashiness. The kind of general junkiness in which I felt most at home with. Weeks' worth of fast food containers rustled and swirled in the floorboard and across the seats as I rolled down the windows and started my way down the dirt road that led away from the ancestral estate. There were even a couple of halfway decent cassettes in one of the cup holders. I snagged out an old Ozzy tape and pushed it in the player. I do love some old school metal on occasion.

I made sure to creep slowly past Granny's, though my instincts were to punch it in case she were to wander onto the porch. The family had discovered over the years that it just did not do to draw Granny's eye until fully prepared. There was only one light on in the tired looking antebellum home in which she resided, and though I was sure I saw a flicker of movement, I steadily just attempted to ignore it.

It was fully dark now, but the full moon coupled with the van's headlights illuminated things just fine. With the windows down, I could feel just how brisk the night air had gotten, the wind blowing across my skin, raising up the hairs there. To my drug-addled mind, it felt like fingers running up my arm and through my hair.

I made it down the driveway from the homesteads and turned onto Old Ebenezer Lane. The dirt road made for slow going at first, as it would not do to start this adventure with running off into a ditch and having to get Uncle Raymond to pull me out with the tractor. The road had been scraped somewhat recently, leaving all manner of rocks kicked up and making the going more bumpy than it usually was. Soon enough, however, I was moving along at a steady clip.

The trees grew close to the road here, creating a tunnel of overarching limbs that blocked out most of the moonlight. The banks were high on either side, the road having worn a deep cut over its many decades of use, and you could see roots spider-webbing through the thick red clay to either side, if one was so inclined. I had spent many an hour doing just that when I was little, looking for ammonites and such. I once had a collection of several dozen fossils that I had pried out of the soil around here. Lidda had gotten most of it as presents during high school, so lord only knows where they are now. But I still have a few of my favorites tucked away back at my shed. Useful little buggers sometimes.

I weighed going back to my shed first, debating on if I needed to gather up some curse-breaking type items, but in the end I decided against it. The plan of attack would be to go refill my box of oblivion at Jimmy's now that I had a decent chunk of change. I would likely end up spending most of the night there, if history was any sort of indication. Then in the morning, I would head out to the pinpointed area and start to do a little snooping. With a little luck, come tomorrow night I might be back in my shed, tweaking out of my ever loving mind having put this whole thing to bed.

I was nearing the edge of our land, rounding a corner of the dirt road when I spotted it. All bleached bone and gnarled root, it looked down from atop the bank at me, the moon giving its skull a dull glow as it turned. I shuddered as it looked at me, and then, thankfully, I was past.

I shook for a good five minutes after I had reached the paved road. It had been a while since I had seen it. I had forgotten how close the old witch house came to the road at that point, a mistake I wouldn't make again soon, at least not after dark. As the shakes subsided, I turned the wheel towards Jimmy's. But I won't talk about that little stop too much. No one likes snitches.

7. New Day Dawning

Jimmy's had proven to be a resounding success. I probably wouldn't sleep for two, maybe three days now, and I could feel the energy coursing through my veins like a stampede of horses. The sun was just starting to come up when I slipped once more behind the wheel and waved goodbye to my second favorite person in the world.

Jimmy stood there in a grimy pink bathrobe and his tighty whities and waved back. He turned back to his camper then, while crushing the beer can in his hand and tossing it onto the mountain of empties he was always saying he would one day recycle. "One day" hadn't come in the four years I'd been coming by, and I suspected it never would.

Threading my way through the half dozen junk cars that filled the yard around the tiny camper, I rolled the window down. The air was cool on my body, and the way the wind coursed over my skin felt like thousands of tiny feather-soft snakes trying to give me hugs. The very air felt electric, and it was one of those mornings that you could just about see sound and hear color if you cocked your head just right. Those of us on a variety of drugs could even skip the head-cocking.

The morning mist was starting to thin a bit as I turned onto county road 98 towards Bay Houdan. It had been a few years since I had been out this way, as I mostly spent my time in Elk Grove these days. I am, and will always be, a child of the country, but small city life suits me just fine. Hard to go without the convenience once you become accustomed to it. And not having to have a car, with all its assorted expenses is always a bonus.

That said, as the cool breeze blew through my hair, I acknowledged that there was something soothing about a drive through the sticks. Having control of where you go, and when. A body could get used to it, that was for sure.

I had the map which contained the closeup of the area spread out on the seat beside me. One end flapped in the wind, but the other was held down by my box of fun. One hand on the wheel, I pressed the flapping end down and gave the map a quick look-over. I had decided to start near the middle of the circle, as that was likely the source of it all, so I would need to turn up Bienville Road once I reached it. Till then though, I just leaned back, flicked a cigarette alight, and cruised.

I decided to take the long way there. Partly because I was not too eager to get to where I was going, but also because I decided it would be best to get a little gas. Not too much, mind you, H.D. had been well-trained at this point to expect me to bring his van back more or less running on fumes. I hate to defy expectations, so a couple of gallons would be enough I hoped. As an added bonus, I could perhaps do a bit of reconnoitering.

Winding my way down county road 98, I turned off onto 7, which looped around to the back side of Bay Houdan if you followed it far enough. Instead, I veered off onto the Jackson Hollow Road after about three miles, and promptly found myself pulling into the Jackson Hollow One Stop.

Jackson Hollow was not a town, community, or anything really. It was a gas station, and the home of the man who owned the gas station. Thirty years ago, he seemingly had the mindset of "if you build it, they will come." Folks said he wanted to be a mayor one day. Surprisingly enough, one gas station on a narrow country road is not quite a mecca for people to move to, and so Terry Jackson and his wife barely managed to eke out a living running the station.

I liked it though. Enough so that it was about the only gas station in the county that I had never even so much as shoplifted a cold beer from. There were always a couple of old men lingering about gossiping, which added credence to its country store credentials, I felt, and today was no exception.

Pulling up to the only pump, I got out and nodded to the pair of elderly black gentlemen seated on milk crates by the door. The One Stop was also the only station in the area that was not pre-pay, so I started to put a couple gallons in as I glanced around. It was a small wooden building, its boards weathered and in dire need of a good pressure washing. Its pair of small windows were filled up with signs for cigarettes.

Gas pumped, I walked inside. Terry's wife, Emma, a short, broad woman with a cheerful smile, was behind the counter. "Howard! Been a while! Been keeping your nose clean?"

I laughed, and gave her what I thought to be a rather roguish wink. "Oh, you know, clean enough, I suppose." I went over to the shelf and scooped up a can of boiled peanuts. "Where are you hiding Terry at today?"

Her face sobered a bit, but she plastered on a smile regardless. "Oh, you know, up at the hospital getting his treatment."

Inwardly, I blanched. I had forgotten he had lung cancer.

A hint of desperation entered her voice. "I took him by to see your granny a week or so back. She was out though. Know when she might be home again?"

When folks tried to get up with my gran, you knew things had gotten bad. I set down the peanuts along with a glass bottle coke. "Granny was home last night. Heard she's been on a bit of a tear though, so I might hold off a couple days."

She nodded, biting her lower lip. "I'll do that." She rang me up and made small talk, clearly eager to veer the topic away from her dying husband. I was just as eager to step back outside and out of there. As the door shut behind me, I opened the can of peanuts and started to drain the water out of it onto the gravel.

"Hull them nuts and drop 'em on in that coke. You'll thank me later," offered one of the old men from off to my left. His hands were wrapped tight around the head of a cane which he was gently rocking side to side between his legs.

I nodded, taking a step closer to them, signaling I was going nowhere in a hurry. "Ain't telling me nothing I don't already know there. I'll drop a few in for sure."

"Hard to beat peanuts and coke," opined the other old man. He was wearing a black "Korean War Veteran" hat which he had tipped pretty far back on his head. "Been doing it since I was a young'un."

I smelled an opening. "Speaking of, how're the peanuts doing this year? Gonna make a good crop?"

Both men hawked and spat so close together you would have thought they had choreographed it. Veteran hat snorted. "All depends on the rain. I mean, they gonna make, regardless. But if folks around here keep having to run the irrigators, ain't no one gonna make any money."

The other man gestured with his cane off to the east. "The Morris boy, he's prolly about ruined at this point. Know him?"

I shook my head.

"Carl Morris' boy. Inherited the farm from old Carl when he passed last year. Small place, can't afford no fancy irrigator. I expect he's about done in. Shame, place been in that family a hundred years. Reckon the bank'll take it now."

Red hat piped up. "Yeah, he had hired a few high school boys to help him try to water with hoses and buckets. But they quit after a couple days. Them buckets get heavy after a bit, and boys these days are just slap full of quit. All account of them participation trophies and such nonsense." He eyed me over, no doubt trying to see if I had just such a trophy sticking out of my pocket. "If you looking to earn a few bucks, might head out that way, haul some buckets."

"You know," I said. "I just might be. Where did you say that farm was?"

8. Farm Day

A dust billowed up from behind the van, turning its white sides red, as I trundled my way down some nameless dirt road. Well, it surely had a name, but some enterprising kids seemed to have stolen all the signs off of it to decorate their rooms no doubt.

There are not that many forms of entertainment for the youth of Jubal County.

To my left was a large field packed with yellowing peanut plants, a sure sign it was getting close to time to pick them. I suspected within the week that field would be dug up, its buried wealth filling the pockets of some farmer. I could see the long, wheeled tubes of the irrigator lording over the rows like some sort of metal dinosaur.

Passing the crops, I made my way further down the narrow road, driving past a number of farms along the way. Cattle stood in drought stricken pastures, eating from hay bales since there was not enough grass to feed them. I saw a goat farm with a pond all but dried up, the goats standing in the sunbaked mud to take sips from the silty water that was left. Things had gotten woefully bad here.

You would think that word of this would be the talk of the county. But in my years, I had found that in matters like this, well, the eyes of the world seem to drift and slide right over them. Folks can tell when something just isn't right, and their minds do their best to hide it from them. Call it a defensive mechanism. Hear no evil, see no evil.

For people like me, you could taste the wrongness of it all. Like an oil slick on water, there was a griminess to the air. A hint of sulfur filled your nostrils, and your tongue felt oily and thick. It was not at all pleasant. The air was thick and dense, and if I had a proper read on it, it was filled with an angry sadness so thick you could practically take a bite of it, though it would have been bitter and you would have spat it right back out.

I spotted a peanut field whose plants had never really reached anywhere close to full size, the bulk of which were a sickly yellow and brown. No irrigator climbed the horizon, so I knew I had reached the Morris farm.

Pulling into the drive, I guided the van up next to the farm house, an old blue painted building, gone a bit grey with dust. The yard was dead, but otherwise tidy, and I was greeted by a trio of rangy mutts who romped up to the side of the van, barking all the while. A hundred yards away, I could see what had to be the "Morris Boy," though he was taller and broader than I was, making his way up a row and pulling a water hose behind him.

I could see that close to the house the plants had reached size, but the farther from the house you got, the worse they became. I imagined that most of the plants were dead and beyond saving, but I had to admire the man for trying, futile an effort as it was. From the looks of things, if he managed to save a fifth of his crop, I would be surprised.

Getting out of the car, I reached my hands out to the bounding mutts. Two immediately shied away still barking, but the third, a tan little thing gratefully took my offered petting. Seeing that I was no threat, and that they were not intending to rend me limb from limb, the four of us set out across the yard into the field, eyeing each other all the while.

Morris the younger just kept watering his peanuts, watching me as I walked up. "They won't bite. But I reckon you know that by now."

Stepping carefully over a row, I extended my hand. "I figured as much. Howard Marsh."

He traded the hose into his off hand, and with his free hand engulfed mine in a too-firm shake. "Eric Morris. Pleasure. Now, what brings you out my way today?"

"Some gentlemen told me you was looking for folks to do a little labor, haul buckets an' the like."

Eric shook his head. "Maybe a bit earlier in the season I would have hired you. But at this point it's a lost cause. I'm just trying to get enough so that I can keep the house at this point, but the rest of the land will most likely get got by the bank."

I shook my head sadly, though inwardly I was a bit relieved. To be fair, I am not the least bit afraid of hard work, and had he offered me work I would have taken it. But I had a feeling hauling water buckets would have put a real damper on the high I was still feeling winding its way through my veins. "Sorry to hear that...wish I could help."

Eric just nodded. "Just ain't been my year." He paused, opening his mouth as if to say something, but clearly he thought better of it and closed it.

That just wouldn't do. I bent over, and took a little pinch of soil between my fingers, using the act to hide a few deft motions with my other hand. I could feel a bit of my high damper off, as that excess energy turned into something...eldritch. Eric gave his head a little shake, as if a fly had just buzzed him.

"What were you gonna say, Mr. Morris?"

A half-glazed look came over the man's face. Something as simple as this spell wouldn't pry a secret out, but something he had already considered saying...should work.

"Well, I was just thinking about all the things that've happened. First, Dad dying, then having to call off things with Ellen, now this...it's a lot to put on a man."

"Ellen?" I asked.

A feeling of sadness entered his eyes. "Jaspers. Ellen Jaspers. She was my fiancée. Just after Dad passed...I can't rightly explain it. But the spark left me. So I called it off."

Bingo.

I turned the dirt loose and the look left the man's face. "Well, I hope things turn around for you. Gotta rain sometime."

Morris just looked about dejectedly. "You'd think that," he sighed. Under his breath, I heard him mutter, "You'd be wrong though."

On that cheery note, I said my goodbyes and made my way back to the van.

9. A Thought, A Snack, And A Goat

I hated using cellphones. But times being what they were, life without one was a seeming impossibility, so begrudgingly I dug mine out and gave Rutherford a call. Of course, the man didn't give me his actual number - just his office, but it sufficed. A few minutes on hold later, I learned that Ellen Jaspers cut hair in Sumpville for work, and lived with her mother on Danielsville Road.

Once I got off the phone, I sat there a moment, pondering. A lover scorned was about as common an origin for a curse as you could get. And though the drought was hurting lots of folks, it was definitely hurting Eric Morris a damn sight more than anyone else. Putting the van in drive, I weighed my options. It was getting later in the day, and my high was still crackling through my system pretty apace. I decided it might be best to track down a bite of food, kill a touch of time, and then head over to the homestead, rather than try to catch her at work.

Bouncing down the dirt road, I let my mind chew over things a bit. The only thing not really meshing to me was that Sumpville was outside the circle. The curse might be about Eric, but it wasn't centered on him. Swearing, I stopped the car again and looked the map over. I couldn't be sure till I got there, but it sure enough looked like where Ellen lived was damn near the center of the circle. Something didn't quite click. Biting on the inside of my cheek pretty hard, I put the map down and set off once again.

It would sort itself out. Or it wouldn't. I didn't rightly care too much in that moment.

Right now, I just wanted some hot fries, a snickers, and a blue Gatorade. Those peanuts I had eaten earlier just didn't do the job; I needed a meal a little better balanced. Thankfully, there was a Citgo between me and Danielsville.

And that was how thirty minutes later I found myself with a snickers in one hand/mouth, while I slipped hot fries through a fence to an eager goat. I like goats: they take life pretty easy, like me. So why not reward one with some of my cherished hot fries? If I could teach a goat to do drugs right, I prolly would never need real people for friends again.

So I passed an hour feeding a goat and dreaming of a life without people.

10. Ellen Back

Pulling off into someone's driveway, I got out the other map, the one that zoomed in on the circle and showed the property lines. Up the driveway, I could see an older woman step through her screen door and out onto her porch to stare at me. I ignored her.

I was well down Danielsville Road, and figured I had to be getting fairly close. That slimy thickness was still in the air, but I could tell I was becoming quite used to it. I would have marveled at what the human mind could get used to, but I tried my damnedest to live my life without ever thinking too hard.

All around, the signs of drought were heavy on the ground. The old lady's yard was brown with dying grass, save for a small flower bed which she had no doubt been watering. The surrounding forest, mostly pines and poison ivy from the looks of things, was likewise struggling, a sea of wilted leaves.

Looking closely at the map, I found a roughly twenty-acre plot deeded to a Rachel Jaspers, which would be where I was headed. I had the address written on the back of a receipt of course, so all I had to do was find the mailbox, but I wanted to see how it stacked up to the circle. If it was not the exact center, well, it was damn close. I slipped the car in drive and left the old woman to her wondering.

Even the kudzu was having a rough go of it, I saw. That stuff was about as hard to kill as anything, so if it was wilting, you knew things had gotten serious. Personally, I hated kudzu, having spent far too much of my youth at the edge of yards trying, and mostly failing, to kill it. So I wasn't totally heartbroken by the sight, even as I knew it was my job to put it right.

I hadn't even driven a mile when I saw a crude vegetable stand, with its hand-painted sign that read "Jaspers Crispers." Jackpot.

I pulled the van up across the road where the ruts showed me most folks parked. It was level enough so I didn't have to worry about the van getting stuck. Getting out, I glanced both ways then trotted across the pavement.

The stand was basically just a table under a big beach umbrella. The bright colors of the umbrella, a riot of pinks and blues, stood out dramatically and caught the eye better than the sign did. Stacked on the table were a few baskets and piles of veggies. I could see corn, tomatoes, squash, as well as a few large watermelons that were placed on the ground underneath. Good thing I had just eaten, or I likely would have bought a few tomatoes to munch on.

Behind the table, slowly fanning herself with a magazine was an older woman of about 50. She was rather pretty, I thought, with blonde hair pulled back in a ponytail, and from what I could see, a fairly shapely figure. She smiled as I walked up, with what seemed like roughly a thousand perfectly white teeth. When your teeth look like mine do, good teeth are a bit of an envy button.

"Afternoon," she said with a voice that was smooth as silk. Words just sound better when they thread themselves through good teeth, if you ask me. No grit to get caught on and jumble the edges of words, I suppose.

I wouldn't even dare smile back, it would just ruin the mood. "Almost evening!" I replied cheerfully, hoping that the angle of the sun would preclude her from examining my teeth too closely.

She gave a small laugh, more of a heavy loud breath than anything, but the sun caught her teeth and I was almost dazzled.

Tighten up, Marsh.

She was pointing out a few of the choicer offerings now, and I had to rein in my mind so that I could focus.

"...and I picked those tomatoes this morning, and that corn there is sweet corn, that's real popular these days. So what can I get for you?"

It occurred to me all of a sudden that it was a bit late in the year for some of these vegetables to look so good. I've worked a garden or two over the years, I would know. Was she trying to pass off store bought? "I have to say I am impressed, Mrs.... Jaspers?"

She nodded with a world shattering smile of perfection.

"Mighty impressed. How do you get them so big and ripe this late in the year?"

She laughed for real this time. "I can't reveal all my secrets now, can I? Suffice it to say I have some really good soil. You can actually see my plot over there..." She turned and pointed behind her up the hill.

About halfway up the hill, which was dotted with pines, I could see a large garden plot. At this distance, it was hard to make out more than tall corn stalks, but I could clearly see a lot of green. It occurred to me that the whole hillside was green, which compared to the surrounding area stood out like a sore thumb. A sore green thumb.

"Very nice," I said, beginning to examine some of the goods closely. I had to do something to quit staring at her teeth so that I could focus. That much green...something was up - something unexpected. Was this all a curse after all? I regretted not talking to Gran after all, but only for a split second.

"Jaspers....not kin to Ellen Jaspers by chance, are you?" I asked, knowing full well the answer.

"Yes! She's my daughter. Why, do you know her?" The woman was nothing if not chipper.

"Not well, but she does my girlfriend Toni's hair," I lied. "Toni will be tickled I met you, I bet. She just thinks the world of Ellen."

"My Elle is a sweetheart," the woman beamed. I made the mistake of looking up just then and was almost struck dumb under the visual assault of two perfect rows of ivory.

I decided to go fishing. "Yeah, she is. Toni said it was such a shame about Eric, said the boy was just plain foolish, calling things off like that."

Mrs. Jaspers laughed again. "He was indeed. Worked out for the best though. She met a new man about two months ago, an Air Force officer from up at Maxwell. That man is a doll, treats her like a princess."

"Oh, that's good," I said, though I saw my carefully constructed theory shot right to shit before my eyes. I hunched down to take a closer look at the melons, giving them experimental thumps to test the ripeness, and buy me time to think as well.

She droned on about this officer and I made what were polite, interested noises, I hoped. Meanwhile I did some thinking. The exact center of a drought zone is green. If the curse-on-the-Morris-boy idea was out, as it looked it was, then there had to be something else at play here. I only had to dig a little deeper.

I pulled a crumpled ten from my pocket. "How many tomatoes will that get me?"

"For ten, you can have what's left in the basket there. I was about to close up for the night anyway."

I was unsure as to how you "close up" a table.

"Just gonna leave all this stuff sitting here?"

She chuckled. "No, I'll carry it all back up to the house."

There was a fair bit of items, several trips easily. I saw an opening. "I'll make a deal with you...I can help you carry all this stuff."

Her eye arched. "And in return?"

I winked at her. "What do you reckon, could maybe a watermelon 'fall off the truck.'"

"You've got yourself a deal!" She grinned.

I scooped up a melon and the tomatoes and ran them over to my van, and then came back and helped her pick up all the veggies that were left. Arms loaded down, we set off up the driveway towards the house, making small talk all the while. It was starting to grow a touch dark as the sun began to make its way below the tree line, turning the cloudy sky a pale red.

About halfway up the drive, I saw we were pulling up even with the garden. "Mrs. Jasper, would you mind if I took just a quick peek at your garden?"

I barely managed to dodge that smile of all smiles as she happily assented. "I retired from the state in February, and decided to try my hand at gardening. I needed something to keep my time filled, you know, what with my daughter grown, and my husband passed. Turns out I had a knack for it!"

She did at that. Her plants were all about the biggest, healthiest plants I had seen in many a year. Even this late in the year they were all heavy laden with vegetables, more than any one family could hope to consume. That wasn't what really caught my eye and chilled my blood, however.

"That's quite a scarecrow you have there." Right in the middle of the garden, was a fairly conventional scarecrow, until you got to the head. Where normally there would be burlap and buttons, and perhaps a straw hat, was instead a deer skull. It was painted mostly black and had a number of small stones tied in such a way as to hang from its antlers, like a primitive wind chime. I could see a few swirls of yellow-gold paint in places, though my eyes weren't good enough at that distance to see what they might portend. Nothing good, I was sure.

"Oh that? My sister gave it to me around the same time I started my garden. She was cleaning out her garage and found it. Said her ex mother-in-law gave it to her for her garden. Which I thought was pretty odd, but then Kelly had married into a pretty strange bunch, though I don't remember them that well. I was off at college for most of it."

My stomach sank. H.D.'s first wife had been a Kelly. And I was pretty sure I recognized that craftsmanship. "Well, it is certainly unique."

Goddamn it, Granny.

11. The Thunder Rolled

I lay on the hood of the van, my back against the windshield staring up at the night sky. Thunder was rumbling in the distance, and in the horizon I could see lightning arc from cloud to cloud. The air had chilled to the point where I could see my breath; little puffs of air that blended with the smoke of my joint.

I'd spent a good bit of time on the phone, till I used up the last of my minutes actually. I had called Rutherford first and informed him of exactly what I thought of his job, and where he could shove it. We finally came to terms when he agreed to not send me back to jail, and to also triple my rate.

I figure my life is worth at least three grand. Well, maybe only two. But a tip is always nice.

After that, I had called H.D. I ended up staying on the phone with him as long as I could, trying to figure out what grinder I was about to stick my dick into. One simply did not mess with something Granny had done all willy-nilly.

I was not 100% certain, but I was almost sure that within that totem acting as a scarecrow head, my gran had bound a Pooka. Why? God only knows. You didn't ask why

64

Granny did anything. And I damn sure wasn't going to go to Granny and ask her to undo what she had done.

Everything he told me that was useful, if you were to write it out, could have fit in a fortune cookie: Pookas could bring good luck, or bad.

Fucking insightful.

Being smart, and knowing his mother, he'd smartly taken the skull and sealed it up in a cardboard box and then crammed it in the back of the garage. Totems like that tended to draw strength from nature. If it was left inside, in the dark, it would never really kick on, so to speak.

Granny was known for her "canning." Instead of making up jars of pickles, family legend had it that she had a basement full of spirit jars, just waiting there in the dark for her to find a use for them. H.D. and I had argued over the years if that was true or not, but no one ever went into the basement, and it was a pretty much a moot point really.

When they'd split, H.D. had long forgotten about the skull, and moved out leaving it behind. I was in the middle of cussing him out for being so stupid when the minutes ran out. It left me feeling mighty unfulfilled to be cut off mid-rant like that. I was feeling ornery, and the joint wasn't really helping to calm me down as much as I would have thought.

Probably had something to do with the assortment of other drugs I had taken in anticipation of the night's shenanigans.

H.D. had mentioned, before the phone had foiled me, that I might want to hold off on putting a stop to things as a storm was riding in. I was none too anxious to tangle with this Pooka, but then I also really wanted the shit behind me, so putting it off wasn't really an option. But that did give me an idea.

I decided to ride down towards the bottom of the drought circle, and pulling off in a little gate area that led into a large hay field, I sat about to watch the storm roll in. I needed to wait until good and late to do what I needed to do, so I had time to kill.

I've always been both partial to and terrified of storms. Did a lot of living in ratty trailers growing up, the kind Tornado Season seemed to love to prey upon, and as a kid I'd spent a lot of sleepless nights praying I wouldn't hear that train sound. But as I got older, I grew to love the look of a storm rolling in, and the sound of rain on tin. I figured this would be a rare treat.

It was too dark to see the clouds clearly. They were dark grey on a black sky, and if it weren't for the lightning you'd never have known they were there. But as I lay there, I could see a half circle of stars blotted out before me, with crackling waves of lightning spreading like tree limbs. I saw one lance out, almost headed straight at me, that slammed to a stop as it hit the edge. The night flared green-gold for a split second, so fast I wasn't sure that it wasn't just a hallucination.

Seeing the storm splayed out like that, it calmed me far better than the weed ever could have. Lying there, I just stared up into the blackness, letting the faint hint of rain-soaked wind edge around my senses. It was a literal calm before the storm, and the irony was not lost on me. I took another long toke on my joint, and settled in to wait.

12. Showdown at High Midnight

It was late, close to 11 or so before I pulled up in front of the Jaspers' driveway, just about in the exact same spot I had been earlier. I looked up the hill and saw the lights were off in the house, so I figured it was now or never. It wouldn't do to try and tackle this thing after midnight.

I eased the car door shut. There was no way anyone in the house could hear a car door shut at that distance, but at this point I was so spooked that I was half afraid I would startle myself if I shut it too loud. I was likely being a bit foolish, but I was so high strung on my bits of joy and oblivion from my box that who could say what I might do. I certainly couldn't.

I leaned against the van, plotting my next move.

I would have to go it alone, I knew that. Reaching in my pocket, I pulled out the little baggy of dried mushroom caps. Without a pause, I turned up the bag and let the taste of earth - and very likely cow shit - hit my tongue. It was gritty to chew, what with all the dirt, but also somewhat gooey in texture.

Once I had swallowed the foul tasting lot, I started slowly up the hill. I took my time, waiting for them to kick in before I got too close. Without them, it was iffy that I would be able to see the Pooka clearly once I called it out, and that would make a dangerous situation even more so.

Clearly, the thing had grown settled where it was, and would be loath to leave. I imagined that if I looked closer at those weather reports, the circle started a bit small and steadily grew till it reached the current size. My guess was that this Pooka had grown attached to Mrs. Jasper, and had decided to kill off the local competition. Or maybe it was leaching the life from the area to fuel her garden. Maybe it was both. Pookas were canny creatures, and mighty spiteful unless they liked you, which was rare. She was lucky.

I also knew that tradition said that after November 1st, food left in a garden belonged to the Pooka, which more often than not meant spoiled, poisoned food. Maybe that was its plan. Grow a good late season garden and poison a bunch of folks. Who knew? Regardless of what it had planned, I would put a stop to it. Or maybe it would kill me.

I had taken enough drugs that I was plenty fueled, and these 'shrooms should do me right up. In a few minutes, I would be a first class Pooka wrangler, I hoped.

The night was fairly cold, and I found myself wishing I had brought a coat or remembered what I had done with my shirt. It was one of my best, and I really hoped I hadn't lost it. I still had my pants and boots though, and really what more do you need, at least until winter came. Besides, I had a bevy of drugs wrapping me up in a warm embrace, paired with a few shots of cheap whiskey.

I decided to lean against a tree just on the edge of the garden and wait on the drugs to take full effect, all the while listening to the night sounds. It was calm out, with a bit of breeze easing through the trees causing a little rustling. There were the usual sounds of crickets and frogs, and at least one obnoxious cicada out there somewhere, but nothing that really stood out. Just normal night noises. The moon was about half full, which gave me more than enough light to watch that totem from where I stood.

The thing seemed to suck up the moonlight, drawing it in like some sort of reverse light bulb. It was like a swirl of shadow there amidst the rows of corn, fighting not to be seen. It was hard, but I could see the rocks and crystals hanging from it swaying gently. It took me a minute of staring, and as I watched, I was a bit unnerved to notice they were swinging across the breeze, not with it.

When it turned to face me, I knew that things had gotten real. So to speak.

When you're sensitive to the other world like me, all it takes is some good hallucinogens, and suddenly you can see the domain of the supernatural pretty clearly. Well, as clearly as staring into a world where shit frequently tends to not make tons of sense.

The hard edge given by the meth was being dampened by the 'shrooms. Around me, colors seemed to slowly fade in and out, pulsing like a slow heartbeat. As the world oscillated from full color to shades of grey, I edged closer to the garden. The skull was still facing me, holding perfectly still, but I knew the Pooka was watching.

I could feel a tingle on my chest, and the brand there began to itch. I resisted the urge to scratch it, instead focusing on the skull. From the bottom of my eyes, I could see my chest start to glow a bit, a sure sign of having drawn the eye of something supernatural. It was nothing you could have seen without the 'shrooms, but in that eerie spirit world the brand began to glow gold. Never a good sign.

Flexing my fingers a little, I took a deep breath to calm myself, and then stepped into the garden. I began whispering a few words of Power, repeating the phrase over and over. The words flowed honey smooth over my tongue, filling my mouth with a warm, buttery aftertaste.

I'd never learned much in the old tongue, and I'd forgotten most of what I had learned, but these had proven useful enough to remember. The words were the supernatural equivalent of "who's a good boy," which I hoped would keep the Pooka calm until I could get a proper handle on the situation. The thing didn't leap out of the skull and try to kill me, which maybe was a good sign. Or it could mean that the spirit was so entwined with the earth that it couldn't bear leaving its totem.

I really hoped it was the former.

Every step was like walking through a wall of static electricity, and that oily, grimy feeling was growing thicker. As my heart began beating faster, the meth coursing through my body had me all but twitching. I was so on edge. I needed to burn off some of this energy soon, or I was gonna be in a bad way. My fingers were flicking overtime, limbering themselves up and warming against the chill.

A feeling engulfed my mind slowly, but there was power behind it. There were no words, at least none that I could have understood, but the intent was violently clear. *Leave.* I stopped moving, and stopped my mantra.

A few words and a backhanded flick of the wrist later, I could see the beginning of glowing threads coming from the skull. My spell would show me pathways of power, which I hoped would let me gauge how embedded to the land this thing had gotten.

Like the spreading roots of an oak, I could see the green bands of magic flow out from the skull into the garden. They spider-webbed outwards, filling half the hillside. I swore. It was dug in deep, like crazy magical tick.

Should I have done this sooner, so I'd have had a better idea of what was going on? Probably would have been the smart thing. But drugs are great for fueling spells, not for thinking clearly.

That intense feeling of "get the fuck out" came on more forcefully now. The feeling came quicker, and with a touch of force that felt like a slight slap. It was growing angry. So I did the metaphysical equivalent of rolling up a newspaper so as to bop it on the nose, and began calling up the Power in a big way.

I had only barely started when thick roots shot up from the ground and wrapped themselves around my ankles. Before I could even squawk, they had me on the ground and were dragging me towards the skull. Thankfully, the tilled soil was soft, but it still knocked the breath from me.

I saw roots shoot up through the scarecrow forming some sort of crazed muscular system for the Pooka, splitting its clothes and enabling it to stand on its own and stride towards me. It grew to at least nine, maybe even ten feet in height, and a baleful green glow came from the eyes of the skull as it powered in my direction. Even more worrying was how the roots that formed its arms were knotting into massive fists.

Fear and lack of breath had slowed me, but as it dragged me close, I managed to flick my fingers in a familiar pattern. Useful for lighting cigarettes, but when coupled with a meth-fueled energy...

Flames burst from the roots around my ankles, and they quickly recoiled. I got a fair nasty burn on my left leg as it happened, sending pain shooting through me, but I could worry about that later. I managed to scrabble to my feet just in time to leap out of the way of the gnarled fist that pounded a brace of cabbages deep into coleslaw.

I don't know how a skull snarls, especially one with no lungs, but I swear that thing made some sort of noise of intense displeasure. We stood a half dozen feet apart, it towering a good half again as tall as me, glowering at each other. I had more Power, but it certainly had home field advantage.

I muttered some words and motioned with an elaborate twist of the fingers a more complex version of my cigarette lighting spell, and a ball of deep blue fire appeared in my left hand. The world had faded all to grey, with the only color being my fire, and its eyes. It looked like something out of a comic book, to be honest, two superheroes all squared off at each other. Only instead of Batman, you got me, a squirrelly little meth head with a snarky attitude.

Now fire could no more hurt a spirit than water could me, but it certainly could light that whole damn garden ablaze in a heartbeat so that Pooka held back, eyeing me over.

"You had a good run. Time to come on back home now though, before you cause any more trouble. I'll make sure you get a few melons on the first. Fair?" I knew it wouldn't understand the words exactly, but it would read the gist from my mind and tone.

It decided to reply in the Old Tongue, which I understand about as well as it understands modern English. Only I ain't got the telepathy to roust out a gist of a meaning. At least not without a good bit more of the right drugs. At a guess though, from the way it was swinging its great big honking fist at my head, the spirit did not much think that was a fair offer.

That fist came barreling towards me, and without missing a beat, I swung my left hand out and met it head-on.

My arm shuddered under the impact, and my shoulder pretty much came out of the socket, but the Power was filling me up hot and heavy now, and with the cocktail of drugs coursing alongside it, it would serve to hold my body more or less together in one piece. At least till the energy ran out.

As the flame engulfed Pooka's hand, it tried to pull away, but was too late. The magical fire rapidly spread up its arm, catching the rest of its body on fire. The smell of burning moldy denim and tubers filled my nostrils, a surprisingly unpleasant odor to say the least. I didn't have time to really take in the scent though, as a mental wail of anguish filled my head, causing me to flinch back.

The makeshift body kept trying to regrow itself, but as quickly as it would grow, the fresh growth would catch alight. The damn thing was spinning like a top trying to put itself out, and in the process was spreading the flames across the garden patch. I had to jump back to avoid getting caught in the middle of it all.

The body collapsed, the skull coming free and falling to the ground. I tried to grab it, but there was a goodly bit of fire between me and the totem, which held me up. Of course, the damn thing decided that it was time to beat a hasty retreat. I suppose it decided freedom outside of Granny's cellar was worth giving up the garden for.

An ethereal body wisped into existence beneath the skull. In a moment, a deer stood before me, or at least a rough, see-through green approximation of one with a jet black skull for a head. It turned to leap away, and I knew if it reached the woods it was as good as gone, and I would never catch it.

Sprinting, I did my best impersonation of a star linebacker and dove for the thing. Had it been sprinting straight away, I would likely just have fallen into a flaming tomato plant. Luckily, it had veered just enough in my direction that I was able to snag one antler with my hand. Putting all my weight into it, I tried tugging it to the ground, pulling it along after me as I fell. Instead, I just hung there a moment, my feet barely touching the ground. And then it took off running anyway, with me being dragged along so fast my feet kept leaving the ground.

We were headed for the woods, where I was sure it had every intention of slamming me into trees till I was either dead or turned loose. I wasn't about to let that happen if I could help it. It was now or never, so with a yell, I buried my heels in the ground, and calling up the Power, let its drug-fueled strength fill my arms.

With a deafening pop, the skull came off the body, which instantly disappeared. The sudden lack of momentum caused me to slam face first into the ground, dazing me badly. Luckily, I kept hold of the skull, and before it could pull any other shenanigans, I sent a blast of power strong enough to hopefully stun the Pooka. It likely wouldn't last long, but it would last long enough for me to get the fuck out of there.

Rising to my feet, I decided, after seeing the lights coming on inside the house, to beat a hasty retreat, before I got arrested for arson. Racing down the hill to the van, I tossed the skull in the passenger seat and dove behind the wheel.

13. Road Tripping

I made it maybe a mile down the road before I realized I had made a tragic error: I was far too high to drive. Tragically so. I pride myself on knowing my limits, and while as your typical south Alabama degenerate I have never been above driving a little under the influence as my revoked license will attest, I do try to limit that as much as possible. I mean, I'm no great shake at driving sober, much less filled to the brim on hallucinogens.

I couldn't linger too close though, as I figured that even then some poor guys were being roused to race over to the volunteer fire department. If they weren't quick, and that fire spread to the dry parts that butted against that pretty green yard, then they'd have a real job ahead of them. Regardless, I needed to get out of sight, and quick.

It's hard to drive when the dividing line on the road gets all curly, twisting around like a snake on a hot plate. I felt like I was driving something like a million miles an hour, hugging curves and squalling tires. When I happened to glance down at the speedometer, I saw, through the swirling orange glow, that I was going maybe fifteen.

This would not do.

I turned up the first side road I saw. It was like threading a needle with yarn, and I may have perhaps missed slightly. The van shuddered and jolted as my wheel dropped off into what was likely a ditch of some sort. There was a rattle, the sound of maybe a hubcap coming off, but who's to say there had ever been a hubcap there to begin with. I certainly couldn't. You couldn't either. No one knows nothing.

I was on a dirt road, a small one, narrow and thin. I didn't need to go down the full length of it though; in fact, the way the trees that lined the road were swaying and sorta reaching for me, I decided it might be best to just stop where I was. Cutting the car off, I sat there, settling down as best as I could for things to simmer down.

I could feel the Pooka stirring beside me. Nothing was actually moving of course, it was more of a general feeling I had. I turned in my seat, looking over at my erstwhile passenger.

For the first time, I was able to really take a good look at it. It had been painted black, then someone had gone over bits of it with a dark yellow spray paint. To call it gold would be a lie - it was too dinghy for that, too...idle. The tips of each antler were yellow, and the bottom of its long face was as well. They'd then painted a looping spiral in almost that exact same yellow color smack dab in the middle of the skull.

I knew the spiral. What it meant.

I could see the hint of that spirit lurking inside that skull, a faint glow that curled at the edge of my vision, like smoke in the wind. While all other colors seemed open to interpretation at that moment, thanks to the coursing hallucinations, the skull itself was rock solid. It was, ironically, an anchor of reality in that moment, a grounding in the world of the spirits.

The bits of rough string that hung from the antiers rustled and shook slightly. Each ended in some sort of trinket, be it a small crystal, a key, or things pertaining to that size. They rattled as the Pooka slowly roused itself up from where I had stunned it. I was a little worried, but I knew I had it out from its "home turf" now, out of that garden. It was less powerful separated from the earth like that.

"Look here now," I said. I let my eyes focus on the skull, helping me keep it together. "We can do this the hard way, or the easy way. If you behave yourself, I'll make sure you get some blackberries. They're good and ruined, just like you like 'em."

I swear that thing hissed at me.

"It's like that then is it," I said, cracking my knuckles in what I hoped was an ominous manner. I was about to thump that sucker once more 'gain, when something struck my window. I let out a little scream, about jumping out of my skin, much less my seat.

"Mighty jumpy there, son. You aight?" said a wrinkled face standing at my door.

"I...uh..."

The man's eyes narrowed. "You look aight, so fuck are you doing in my driveway? You drunk?" He looked past me into the van, his eyes locking on to the skull. "You doing some sort of voodoo shit in my yard, son?"

"No, sir," I started. I was on tilt, and way too high to be dealing with this. Had I pulled into a driveway instead of a dirt road? That would explain why it was so narrow. "I was just stopping for a second, I was getting sleepy." I was pleased by my quick thinking.

"Well, how about you go sleep it off some'ere else and quit scaring my wife half to death." He tapped the glass again, and I saw he was doing it with the barrel of a small pistol.

"Fair enough," I said. In a lower voice, I muttered, "Mighty Christian of you."

I fumbled a moment or two in the darkness before I was able to get the van running again. That old bastard just stood there in his bathrobe and flannels, giving me the mother of all stink-eyes. I had half a mind to slip it into drive and give him a scare, but being this high, and knowing my luck, I'd run the old bastard over. I'm a lot of things, but I have never killed anybody, and I didn't aim to start now.

Looking in the rearview mirror, I knew there was no possible way I was going to be able to back down that driveway. So seeing a gap, I hauled off and did a fairly admirable three-point turn in that prick's yard. I heard some sort of thunk along the way, and I was fair certain from his yelling that I'd damaged something. Well, I figured it served him right for bothering me like that.

Beside me, the skull was just quivering. It was sure enough rousing itself up to try something, but unless I wanted a few shots popped off in the van, I needed to get elsewhere. Worse, the old man might call the cops on me. They'd sure enough be in the area, what with the fire, I reckoned.

"Be easy now," I said to the Pooka as I reached the paved road once more. I had to wait for a car to pass, but luckily, it was headed in the same direction I wanted to go. I figured it would be easier to follow it than to just wing it. But I took so long to get good and going that it had disappeared around a curve before I could roll along behind it. If it had ever been there in the first place.

As best as I could, I kept my eyes peeled for the brilliant green of my headlights shining off a street sign. Jubal County had been eaten up with little side roads, and thanks to that E-911 deal they put in a few years back, they all had names and signs now. So long as some kids hadn't come along and stolen them, that is.

Somewhere between a mile and an eternity, I spotted a blessed snippet of green that read...something. The letters had sorta all melted and ran together, at least that was how it looked in my almost dead eyes. It damn sure wasn't a driveway though. I grinned as I turned onto its broad dirt expanse.

My grin shattered as the passenger window cracked. A spider web spread across it, dozens of small cracks threatening to shatter it. I felt the Pooka as it did it, a sort of electric whoosh that filled the air a split second beforehand. The damn thing was trying to break out.

Slamming on the breaks, I threw the van in park, then called up the Power. A glowing electric buzz filled my soul, and I thumped my hand down on the skull. The damn thing should have been turned into powder. Instead, my hand came away red and stinging. Whatever Granny had spelled into that skull was damn solid.

The Pooka slumped back into whatever spirits did when you effectively knocked them out. I'd put a good bit more power into this blow, which would keep it settled long enough for me to sober up. At least sober enough to drive safe. Well, safer.

Using the Power like that, it burned up a chunk of my high, so to speak. I had to dance a fine line though. I could easily just cast a bunch of stupid spells, and then burn myself clean and sober. But then I'd be toothless if the Pooka woke up before I could get it to Granny's. So I got the van pulled a bit more out of the way than it had been, and settled down for my brain to settle down.

Then it started raining.

14. Pitter Patter, Let's Get At Her

Time had a funny way of moving, but the clock told me that about an hour had passed by the time I felt able to take on the world. I had no doubt there would be moments of flashback and skullfuckery, but I was cooking along on a fairly even keel finally. Reality had taken on a sort of firmness to it that I found simultaneously pleasing and disappointing.

I was pretty sure the Pooka was awake, but it was minding itself, and not causing any sort of ruckus. I guess that last smack had done the job and it was set to behave now. If not, well, I could always just swat it again, I figured.

At some point, I couldn't now recall I had buckled up the deer skull, threading the seatbelt across its horns. Whether that had something to do with its current quiet state I couldn't guess, but it seemed best to just leave things as they were. Glancing at the cracked window, I figured at least this way it couldn't go leaping out if the window finished shattering. I looked close to see if any rain was leaking in, and so far at least there was none.

This was the surest sign that I had set things right, I supposed, the fact that it was now raining inside the area that had been a drought zone. I reckoned if I could have been watching a weather radar it would have shown that the storm had stopped flowing around that circle and started flowing right over it. It tickled me to no end, as I imagined the money I was soon to be receiving. Rutherford would be happy, I assumed, if the man was capable of an emotion other than "prick."

I was less pleased to find that my uncle had gone quite some time without replacing his windshield wipers. They were barely able to keep up with the falling rain, and did a better job of smearing the water rather than actually slinging it off the glass. If it started coming down way harder, I was gonna be pissed.

I had gotten my bearing, and knew my whereabouts. I could just follow down the dirt road I was parked on, and in a few miles it would come out on highway 98. That would have me good and on my way.

The thirsty dirt of the road was quickly soaking up the rain. The occasional burst of lightning came on now, fighting my headlights for the task of lighting my way. There were mostly just cow pastures on either side of this little road, and in my few glances left and right I could see the cattle hunkered down, small black mounds dotting the cleared land. I was sure glad not to be in their shoes.

I had made it to the end of the road where it T'd into 98 when that skull gave a crackle of activity. I stopped, looking at it hard, even as I started to call up a flicker of power. Before I could act, however, the totem pulsed green, bright enough that it partially blinded me for a moment. Then it happened.

A torrent of filth spewed from where the deer's mouth would have been. It was a river of rotted vegetables and fruit, runny with sour decay. It fountained out, striking the dash before cascading into the floorboard. Chunks of putrid plant matter splattered everywhere.

The smell was something that will always haunt me. I have never smelled anything so foul, so withering. The stench of death was entwined with the reek of decomposition, filling my nose and leaving me gasping for breath. It was so noxious I swear it was actually roasting the hairs inside my nose.

Desperately, I rolled down the windows, not giving a flying fuck about the rain. I gasped hungrily at the rain-tossed air that flowed in, desperate for something actually breathable. I was so caught up trying to remain alive that I almost didn't hear it.

click

I wheeled to see the seatbelt coming unfastened. The soiled mess had thankfully stopped flowing from the totem's mouth, though a huge puddle several inches deep now filled the floorboard on that side. Lunging, I reached across and snapped the buckle back together with one hand, as with my other I rolled up the passenger side window. I had to hold my breath as I did so: so acrid was the air.

Soon as that was done, I leaned my head out of the window, letting the rain pelt my face as I breathed deeply. From the corner of my eye, I watched the damned thing, but it just sat there. Clearly, its plan now was to drive me out of the van so it could escape. Well, the joke was on it. While this was easily the most disgusting smell I had ever encountered, I typically lived in a general state of filth. It was going to take more than a bad smell to run me off.

Carefully reaching out, I wrapped my hand around the seat belt clasp, and with a few words I melted it beneath my hand. Not much, mind you, just enough that it could no longer unclasp, at least not without some serious work.

It suddenly occurred to me that H.D. would probably not be well pleased with the state of his van when I got around to returning it. I'd transcended beyond the usual "leaving it on empty," and had perpetrated a bit of real damage to the thing. I had some vague memories of having perhaps struck a few things while in my higher state, but decided to ignore that for now. The puke was a bigger issue really.

As I stared, I saw a fist-sized fragment of what looked like watermelon rind bubble to the surface, breach for a moment, before being sucked back down into the slimy green sludge. The smell coming from it was still terrible, but with the window down, it was gradually becoming bearable. At least my nose hairs had stopped burning.

I decided against trying to clean it up, at least at that point. I had no doubt Hubert Dale would make some attempt at getting me to clean it later, but for now I concluded that there was no point. What if I went to the trouble of shoveling the bulk of it from the floorboard for it to just repeat itself? Clearly, the size of the skull had zero relevance to the amount of bile that it could produce. No point in tempting fate.

I cracked the passenger window a bit, and with my head mostly out my own window, I resumed my travels.

15. A Minor Hiccup

I figured that I was maybe a twenty-minute drive away from Granny's, assuming the weather didn't get much worse. I ended up having to pull my head in as the raindrops began to sting once I picked up speed. But with that speed came wind, which made having my head inside the van tolerable. I was almost getting used to the smell, at least as used to it as you could get. The roiling in my gut had faded, and the urge to vomit had passed. I could feel that skull just steamin' mad, but it was making no more moves, so I let it be.

The rain was holding steady, my level of high was within the limits, and the van was still running. I had three grand waiting on me, more money than I could ever remember having at one time by far. I'd even gotten laid out of this whole affair. Life was shaping up to be damn fine.

Then I topped the hill I'd been passing up, and my heart stopped.

Up ahead was a roadblock. Through the rain splatter, my eyes filled with a torrent of reds and blues. For a moment, the light was a riot of prismatic color, filling my vision like an avalanche of living blue raspberry slushie. After a second it passed, leaving an echo of that wonder on my retinas to go along with the horrible sinking feeling in my gut.

There was a trio of cop cars, parked along and across the road, leaving a gap big enough for one car to pass through at a time. I'd seen these often enough as a passenger, but had never hit one as a driver. It was a simple license and insurance check. The only problem was I hadn't had a license in years, and if this van was properly insured I would shit gold, not to mention the large quantity of drugs I had on deck.

Or the fucking Pooka.

Without a conscious thought, I whipped the van around, killing the headlights as I did so. I just had to hope they didn't see me. Maybe the rain would do me this one favor, just this once maybe my luck would not fuck me over. I punched the gas as hard as I could and the van lurched forward, getting me behind the crest of the hill so I could cut the lights back on.

My heart was pounding, the wind screaming in my ear through the open window. Or maybe that was me. Maybe it was the Pooka. Things had gotten real out of sorts all of a sudden. It was a hell of a time for lingering snippets of hallucinogens to start firing in my brain. So when the police lights cut on just in front and slightly to the side of me, I prayed for a moment that it was just my drug addled brain messing with me.

This was not the case.

The cop car had been hiding, lying in wait for folks like me who didn't feel like going through the block. Sitting in some driveway, or behind some tree. I don't know where exactly, but as it whipped out into the road behind me I knew all too well just where it was. I thought about trying to outrun the bastard, but then I remembered I was in an aged Astrovan, not a Mustang.

It took me a few moments to convince myself not to try it anyway. In that time, the cop got so close on my bumper I could damn near feel their breath on my neck. Lights were flashing, siren wailing, and speaker blaring. Between the wind, rain, and panic rising up in me, the voice sounded more like the teacher voice from Charlie Brown than anything really human. I knew what they would be saying though, this wasn't my first rodeo.

I pulled off onto what may have been a dirt road, or may have just been a really long driveway. It was hard to tell in the dark, and although it was certainly dirt, it seemed a bit too maintained to be any sort of road left in the care of the county. Trees grew up close to one side, the side I pulled over onto, while the other looked to be open with what might have been a hay field.

The cop car pulled in behind me, squatting ominously. Nothing moved that I could see, and I could only assume whoever it was was running the plates to check for warrants. What it did was drive me almost to the breaking point. I was scared in a way the Pooka had not been able to manage. It was strange; I knew any other day, at any other time, I'd have been running my mouth, flipping the bird, and being a troublesome ass. What was some jail time? I basically had a standing room reservation there.

But in that dark...there was a wildness in me that made me want to run. To dive out the side passenger door and take off running into the woods. To tear off my clothes and run naked beneath the moonlight...what?

I swatted the skull and the rising terror lessened. "Would you fucking stop? I got enough shit to deal with without you riling things up for fuck's sake."

Hearing a car door open, I looked in the side mirror. Out shuffled one of the local sheriff's deputies, pulling on an orange raincoat over their uniform. It was hard to tell, but I thought it was a woman, and as she neared, I saw that was the case. Her skin was dark, so unless the force had gotten some new recruits, I knew it had to be...

"Deputy Williams, evening," I said, putting on my most charming smile. Latoya Williams didn't have the full-on hate for me that most cops seemed to have. She certainly didn't like me, but then I could count the number of folks who did on one hand pretty much. We'd gone to school together from kindergarten till I dropped out. We had even been friends back then for a bit, the way the smart kids would sorta stick together. Those days were long gone, but enough memory lingered with her that she'd sometimes talk first and taze later.

She swore as she stepped towards the window, her boots squelching through the mud. "You didn't hear me telling you to pull over, Marsh?"

"I did, but see, this ain't my van. It's H.D.'s. I didn't want to risk getting it stuck in the rain." The stink of the vomit was rising.

Stepping up, she almost instantly reeled back. "What the hell? What's that smell, Marsh?" She put a hand to her face, covering her mouth and nose. She held up her flashlight, clicking it on. It was one of those long silver Maglites, the kind that could double as a club. Still holding her nose, she shone it inside.

I was opening my mouth to try and bullshit an explanation, but she cut me off. "Get out the van," she said.

Glancing at the skull, I hesitated a moment, then stepped out. My head and shoulder were already wet, so it wasn't a great sacrifice to step out into the rain. I noticed LaToya made no move to provide me any cover. Which I didn't mind. I just noted. Quietly. And to myself.

Away from the van, she was able to uncover her nose, though one knuckle rested on her lips as she made this odd face. It was like she was praying for patience, but all God was sending down was annoyance. It'd have been funny if I didn't suspect it would bode poorly for me.

"Marsh, what the fuck did you eat?" She finally asked as she opened her eyes and lowered her hand.

I raised both hands. "Oh no, that ain't my doing. Honestly, have you ever smelled anything like that before? Anyone that pukes that up has to be dying."

The officer sucked her teeth. "Then what is it? Have you started hauling toxic waste now? Is stealing copper outta ac units not lucrative enough anymore?"

I had no sort of answer that would satisfy her. None. Maybe if I was a little less doped up I could have thought of something. Maybe if the Pooka hadn't tweaked my mind up

96

so hard I could have planned this out better. If wishes were horses.

I shrugged.

"A shrug? That's all you got for me?" She arched an eyebrow. "None of your usual snark and awe?"

"LaToya..."

"Deputy Williams, please and thank you," she said firmly.

"Deputy Williams, you know me. You know good and well I ain't got no license, and most times if you see me out and about, I am up to what most folks would consider no good. You got a rough idea about how much of my life gets spent in the jail. About the shit I get into."

Sighing, I wiped the rain from my face. "You got me driving all sorts of illegally, and even if you was the bribable type, which so far as I know you ain't really, I don't have anything you'd want. You got every right to haul me off to jail."

"But?" She asked. "I feel like there's a 'but' coming."

I nodded. "But this one time, just this once't, I'm asking you to let this slide."

She snorted. "Oh, this I got to hear."

"I mean, it's raining, and I'm sure you'd much rather be back in your car than dealing with me. But you're a decent cop, so you ain't likely to let comfort come before duty. I get that. It's damn near respectable in my eyes." I leaned back against the van door. "But you also caught a whiff of what's inside, and I know good and well you don't want any more to do with that. And if you go to arrest me, you're gonna have to search the van."

It was hard to tell under the hood of her rain jacket, but I think she was arching an eyebrow. "Not good enough," she said, her hand pulling out her handcuffs. "You know the drill."

"Wait now," I said, raising my hand up in front of me, like I was trying to fend off an attack. Which I guess I kinda was, not that most people would view it as such. "Those are reasons, but not the good reasons. I mean, they work plenty fine for me, but then I might be biased."

"Might be?" She laughed.

I winked. "There's a good reason you shouldn't do it, and then there's the real reason. The good reason is because if you arrest me, it's to no point. I'll be out within the hour. One phone call, and I'll be free. I promise you that." I wasn't actually sure if Rutherford would bail me out, but I was sure I could spin him in such a way that he'd get me turned loose, if for no other reason than to make sure the Pooka went back to where it belonged. "You know I got arrested yesterday morning? And here I am, out free and not even on bail. Just turned loose. Same thing'll happen again. So why waste your time?"

LaToya eyed me warily. Stepping away, she never took her eyes off of me, but once she was out of easy earshot she made some call on the radio. It took a minute or so, in which time I just stood there getting steadily more wet. It was a cold rain, and I knew that pretty soon I would be shivering. If I ended up with a fucking cold from all this, I knew I was going to be mighty pissed.

Stepping back, there was a curious look on her face. "So what's the real reason?"

I locked eyes with her, and put on my serious face. I have pretty blue eyes, but when I want, they look cold and piercing, like icy daggers. I met her curious gaze with my forceful one. "Because LaToya there's something going on right now that you want no part of. It's not illegal, I promise you that, nothing that will blow back on you. But it's something you won't believe until it's too late, and then there's no turning back. Something that me and mine are equipped to handle so that the rest of the world don't ever have to know what's really there."

"What do you…" she started to ask.

Cutting her off, I gestured back inside the van. "You saw that skull, and you smelled that smell. That ain't me just gathering up early Halloween decorations. You've heard the rumors about my family, and you're a smart woman. You can put two and two together, but when you get four, just know that it's a four that right now, only I can handle. A four that if it were to get loose, might start adding numbers of its own, only it'd be in dead bodies."

That was a real exaggeration of course, Pookas very rarely killed anyone, at least not directly. But she wouldn't know that, wouldn't even know there was such a thing as a Pooka, and I figured she would spin it in her mind that this was all for the greater good. Whatever it took, I just really wanted to be done with this, and jail would only prolong matters.

The deputy looked from me to the van, and back again. I could see her face was a war of emotions. She really was one of the good ones, which was rare in the Jubal County sheriff's department. She bit her lip, then nodded. "You promise me you're good to drive?"

I raised my left hand, putting my other hand over my heart. I had her. "Scout's honor."

She stood there, staring at me, not saying a word. "What happened to you, Marsh? Why are you like this?" she asked after a few moments. I didn't like the direction this was headed. I wanted to speak, but she raised a hand, and just turned and started to walk away. Pausing, she looked over her shoulder. "You're smarter than this," she added softly. "Get it together, before something really bad happens."

I didn't get back inside the van until she had pulled away. To her taillights, I finally answered. "Why am I like this?" I laughed, but it was bitter sounding, even to me. "Because something really bad happened."

16. Rain, Rain, Take Me On Out Of This Town

Even though LaToya had let me go, I wasn't so foolish as to believe that I would be able to pass through that insurance checkpoint without being hassled and then arrested. Convincing the one deputy who doesn't hate you to give you a break is one thing. Convincing three cars' worth of ones that do hate you is another.

Grumbling all the while, I turned the van down a road that would take me to my destination while avoiding the cops. It was longer, and more out of the way, but I didn't have any choice really. Normally, I would have enjoyed a bit of the scenic route, but it was too dark to enjoy the view, and I really just wanted to go home.

LaToya's surprising care had me spiraling into a bit of a funk. I don't know why I cared what the hell she thought, but I did. Maybe it was because she remembered me back before everything went wrong. Not that things were great even then, but they were better. My brain took to twisting down a path of woulda/coulda/shoulda, and I suddenly found myself aching for a bit of oblivion.

I had my box of oblivion of course, but anything in there would have me riled back up and unable to drive. That was the exact opposite of what I wanted. A few shots of whiskey would have been the ticket, or even a few beers, just enough to help take the edge off. But I didn't have any of that on hand, and I wasn't sure getting even a little drunk was the best move in this sort of weather.

In the end, I decided that fate had shown its hand. The new route I was taking took me right by the Stone Road Shell, which was the only gas station outside of Elk Grove and Sumpville that was open after midnight. Glancing at the glow of the dash, I saw that I could probably stand to put a couple bucks in gas in the tank as well. I didn't want to get H.D.'s expectations up for future times that I borrowed it, but then I figured it might be best to make up for the little bit of damage I had done.

Ten minutes later, I was handing a pimply faced young woman a ten dollar bill in exchange for a Steel Reserve tall boy and some gas. I gave her my winningest smile, which judging from the blank stare she gave me in return, went over like a brick in a Jello pile.

She looked half asleep, which may have explained her not noticing me slipping a few Slim Jims in my pocket. Or maybe she just didn't care. I'd be surprised, judging from her looks, if she was long out of high school.

I stepped outside, peeling the wrapper from a stolen piece of jerky. "Kids these days," I muttered.

The rain was still coming down, but the awning that covered the pumps was keeping it off of me. The shell was an old store, and its owner hadn't sunk any real money in the place in years. A good half of the bulbs were blown overhead, and several of the rest were just flickering. Glancing up, I could see the fixtures hadn't been cleaned in a long time, the bodies of thousands of dead bugs littering the inside of them.

As I started pumping the gas, the wind began gusting, and the rain which had been falling almost straight down began blowing sideways. This had the effect of sending the rain falling on me once again. I swore, but really there was no way I could get much wetter than I already was, thanks to my interlude with the deputy. Luckily, I was only getting about three gallons, so it didn't take long.

Settling back into the van, I pulled the tall boy from the small brown paper bag. I crumpled the paper and flung it into the puddle of vomit. I half expected it to sizzle, or catch fire, but it just began sinking into the gunk, soaking up bile. With a shrug, I popped the tab on the beer and took a long sip.

I'd compromised on one beer. Drugs would have taken me in the wrong direction, there was no place to buy liquor this late, and a whole six pack would have been unfortunate most likely. One beer though, even though it was a big one...well, I needed something to soothe my ache.

I was the only one there at the pumps, so I sat there drinking the beer. I watched the girl through the window. She was partially obscured by a coke ad, but from what I could see, she just hunched there, her head in her hands, fighting to stay awake. She didn't even bother watching the TV, which through the static looked to be playing some sort of late night talk show.

Thinking about the weed, I was sure tempted to walk back in and see if she wanted to smoke a joint. That would do a real good job of taking the edge off, and I really didn't want to be alone just then. I was feeling powerfully lonesome. But then I remembered the fucking spirit in my passenger seat and thought better of it. Sometimes you just had to be alone with your demons, both figuratively and literally.

A huge bolt of lightning struck nearby, startling me. When I glanced back, I saw it had even managed to rouse the young woman, who was now staring out the window. I saw her look towards me. I gave a half-hearted wave, but she just went back to cradling her head.

I downed the last of the beer and flung the empty can out the window, trying to ring the trashcan. I missed by a good three feet, but I didn't have it in me to get out and pick it back up. Deciding to leave it for sleepy beauty to take care of, I slipped the van back out into the storm.

The rain was now really starting to pour. I couldn't in good conscience leave the window down now, as the rain was pounding hard enough that I was worried it might ruin what was left of the ratty interior of the old van. I tried leaving it cracked, but water was still coming in faster than I was really comfortable with.

With the shitty job the old wipers were doing, I had to slow down even more than I had been. The worn blades couldn't keep up, and I was finding it harder and harder to see. I slowed to forty miles an hour, then thirty, then twenty.

It was raining so hard that the water was puddling on the road, and for one butt-puckering moment, I felt the van start to skew, threatening to hydroplane me right off the road. I debated just stopping again, but I was so close to home at this point that I decided to risk it. Lightning was striking with disturbing regularity, getting steadily closer.

I was so focused on the road that I didn't notice the Pooka at first. It was letting loose a low hiss, like a kettle slowly releasing steam. I couldn't spare time looking away from the road, it was too dangerous for that, but I listened as close as I could, and sorta tried reaching out with my other senses, but didn't really get anything.

Coming upon another car, I was left blind by its headlights. The beams struck the poorly wiped water on the windshield and refracted, obscuring all of my view. I pumped the brakes, coming almost to a complete stop as for a moment I lost sight of the road.

Slowly accelerating again, I tried once more easing through the storm.

17. Thanksgiving

It was with a tremendous amount of relief that I finally turned onto the dirt road my family lived on. The rain was coming harder with every passing moment, and the fucking Pooka was hissing louder right along with it. I figured it must have been summoning up that storm, using its magic to manipulate the already existing weather. Stopping it had crossed my mind more than once, but in the end, I figured that I would rather have it focus on making the weather worse, than something I couldn't see coming. Bad weather, I could deal with.

The road was slick and muddy, and I slowed even further. The speedometer was barely moved off of zero, but I only had a few miles left to go, so I didn't care. I kept to the middle of the road, staying as far from the ditches as possible. I could see they were starting to overflow, which was worrisome, but again, I didn't have far to go.

And then there was the turkey.

Why was a wild turkey running around in this sort of weather? It defied all logic. The damn thing should have been roosted up tight in some tree, trying its best to stay dry.

What it should not have been doing was launching itself from one of the high embankments to the other.

Unfortunate for me, and doubly unfortunate for the van, was that the embankments at that point were roughly windshield height. So as it flung itself, wings flapping through the night, it smacked right into the windshield. I shouted, snatching the wheel and slamming the brakes, but it was too late.

The windshield was crushed. It didn't fully shatter inwards, but it was heavily dented in, the center of a spreading spider web of cracks. The turkey itself flew back over the van out of sight, a dust cloud of feathers in its wake. The van, however, didn't stop moving, as it kept sliding through the mud.

I tried cutting the wheel, but it was too late. It was lucky I was going so slow, but regardless the van slipped into the ditch, one headlight going dark with a crunch. It was so slow motion of a wreck that it would have been comical, if I wasn't already thinking of how pissed H.D. was going to be.

I'd been rocked a little, but my seatbelt had held me in place. There hadn't been the speed for whiplash, hell, the belt hardly even locked. Looking at the windshield, I knew it was a wonder that it hadn't completely blown inwards. A face full of glass was not what I wanted, that was for damn sure.

The passenger window finished cracking, and fell outwards. It happened just long enough after the actual wreck that I was pretty sure the Pooka was behind it. There was nothing I could do about it, however, so I just stared at it, mouth agape. My uncle was going to kill me, was all I could think about as rain began pouring in.

Throwing the van in reverse, I tried to back out of the ditch. The tires spun, splattering mud everywhere, but the vehicle didn't move. I turned the wheel every which way, pumping the gas as I did so, but the damn thing refused to shake loose. I sort of lost it there for a minute. Screaming, cursing, fist slamming into things, the works. It was dramatic.

When I calmed down enough to think clearly, I realized I needed to get that side window covered. I could get one of my uncles to come pull the van out, but that would take time. I checked my cell phone and found it was dead as hell, so there would be no calling for help. I would have to walk it. Turning in my seat, I rummaged through the junk in the back of the van until I found an old black trash bag.

Stepping out of the van, I found myself in water so deep that it reached my ankles. This had the effect of allowing muddy rainwater to flow in through my laces, instantly soaking my socks. This did little to improve my mood.

The mud squelched underfoot, and I had to fight at times to keep my feet from slipping. I saw the corpse of the turkey lying in the middle of the road a score of yards away, and walking over to it, I gave it a good hard kick. Wet feathers went flying, and if anything, I felt worse than before.

Stomping back to the van, I opened the passenger door and set about trying to slide that garbage bag in place. It was a pretty snug little space, with not a lot of room for me to get the door open, being so close to the embankment. And the bag was only just big enough that I was able to carefully scooch it down over the top of the door. It eventually got too wide, but the bag covered most of the glassless space, with only about an inch of space left for rain to fall in. That would have to do.

Shutting the door, I turned and my heart skipped a beat. The turkey was gone.

18. Well, That's Not Good

I whipped my head back around and flung open the door. I reached out and put my hand on the totem, sending out a little tendril of power. The skull was empty of any spirit. When I say that I swore, know that this is a horrific understatement.

Slamming the door shut, I ran to where the carcass had lay. There were still a number of feathers lying around to mark the spot, a bit of blood as well, turning the rainwater pink. I frantically began to look around, my eyes darting in all directions.

Movement caught my eye to the right, and looking close, I could see the mangled body of the turkey disappearing into the tree line atop the embankment. It was a hobbling mess, but I was just thankful it wasn't flying. If it had flown off, I would have been well and truly fucked.

I was already moving towards it the moment I realized I'd spotted the damned thing. I was halfway across the road when I realized I would need something to carry the Pooka back in, assuming I managed to catch it.

Racing back to the van, I tugged open the back hatch and began frantically looking for something, anything that was even vaguely like a container. My heart soared when I saw a familiar yellow color, and with a cry of victory, I pulled out an old plastic Country Crock butter tub. It had heft to it, I found, and I popped it open.

I almost gagged. If I wasn't fairly numb to all smells at that point, thanks to the Pooka's vomit, I would have thrown up, surely. There was some sort of moldy mess inside that might have at one time been spaghetti. It was impossible to tell under all the fuzzy blue-green mold, however. I didn't take time to investigate though, I just dumped it empty then took off once more for the embankment.

Splashing through the water of the far ditch, I reached up to grab onto a root to try and pull myself up. My boots struggled to get any sort of traction on red clay hillside, and the root itself was slick with rain. I had to toss the plastic tub up ahead of me so as to be able to use both hands, as my one-handed fumbling wasn't getting me anywhere.

I made it halfway up when my boot, which had managed to get a little grip on some sort of rock, decided it no longer believed in things such as traction. My foot slipped, and my shin crashed into the rock, hitting with enough pain that I let go of the root. I fell into the ditch ass first, splashing into the water like a clumsy kid.

The anger I had felt earlier was a pale shadow to my state of mind in that moment. If I'd had the spell and the power, I'd have burned the whole world to ashes. The rivers would have run red with blood, and frogs would have fallen from the heavens.

I hadn't thought I could really get anymore wet, but falling into a rushing muddy stream proved me wrong. I was soaked from head to taint now, and I could already feel echoes of chafing from the future ruining my night. I'd left my dead phone in my back pocket, and now I was certain it was dead for real. Walmart cheapo phones don't tend to have much resistance to, well, anything much at all.

With a snarl, I leapt to my feet and let my anger propel me up the embankment. I practically floated up on a cloud of barely constrained rage. The recalcitrant earth clearly knew better than to fuck with me now, and my rebellious boots were no doubt in fear for their life, so within seconds, I was atop the bank and scooping up the tub.

I set off into the woods at a trot, following in the direction I'd seen the Pooka/turkey staggering. It would be a good bit ahead, but I knew the condition the van had left that carcass in, so I knew the damn thing couldn't move too fast. If I hurried, I could have it popped out of there in no time.

I'm not sure what, over the course of the past few hours, would lead me to believe that would be the case, but hey, luck's gotta turn sometime. I mean that's what I've heard at least, not that I would really know from personal experience.

Within the woods, the rain was lessened by the tree limbs overhead, but the wind was still whipping the limbs to and fro. Coupled with the frequent lightning strikes, I was a little worried for my health. If the Pooka was manipulating this storm, then who was to say it wouldn't try calling down a bolt of lightning to fry me right up? Though the way the wind was blowing, a falling tree limb seemed just as likely to take me out the game.

Dark forest surrounded me on all sides. I was in the midst of what looked to be mostly pines, and the ground was thickly blanketed with a bed of dead needles. What little undergrowth there was consisted mostly of briar thickets, which I did my best to avoid, but running through the darkness didn't make that easy.

I stopped, looking around me, trying to see if I could spot the pooturka. Mouthing a few words and flicking my fingers, I summoned up a ball of blue flame in the palm of my hand. It didn't do the best job lighting my way, but it was better than nothing. Wheeling around, I caught a glimpse of reflected light coming from a set of eyes near chest level to me.

Hunched on the side of a pine was a squirrel, its rat-like body clinging to the bark, its tail flicking back and forth angrily. Beady little eyes stared at me, and before I could react, the damn thing launched itself through the air at me. Its small mouth was open wide and its tiny little claws were grasping at me as though it aimed to rip my throat out.

Jumping back, I smacked the squirrel out of the air, knocking it to the ground in the process. Its little teeth had hit my hand, leaving a tiny gash I could feel, but the squirrel had gotten the worse outcome. It was dazed, stunned by the force of my blow.

I screamed as something latched onto my calf. Kicking out wildly, I slung another squirrel skyward as it shook loose. It took a small chunk of flesh with it as it hurled through the air. It stopped when it hit a nearby tree. It managed to hang onto the bark somehow, turning and chittering at me wildly.

The one I had dazed was starting to try and chew into my boot now, which caused me to jump back. I could see that there were at least several more fucking squirrels skittering their way down a tree towards me, their beady little eyes all filled with blue flame and mayhem. I have a soft spot for small woodland animals, but fuck those squirrels.

The closest caught an orb of blue flame to the face as I turned and took off running. Before, I'd been jogging, but now, I wanted space between me and those damn squirrels. I called up another orb, feeling it burn through more of my high, using up my carefully hoarded and drug-fueled power. Turning a squirrel into a tiny bonfire was one thing, but doing the same to a forest worth of squirrels...well, I'd need a lot more drugs. And it suddenly occurred to me that I had left my box of oblivion in the van beneath the seat.

A quick glance behind me showed the squirrel-b-que was sputtering out, the tiny rodent having not provided much fuel for the magical flames. In the dying light though, I could see at least half a dozen or more squirrels and wood rats go scuttling past. "Well, that's not good," I muttered, my smoker's lungs protesting at the wasted breath.

19. Boil And Trouble

I held out my hand which held the orb of flame, using it to light my path. It caused shadows to flicker ominously on all sides, and I found myself staring at nothing. I was convinced that every shadow and windblown branch was a rodent hurling itself at me. I'd heard that story about the man who got his nipple bitten off by a beaver. No way in hell was I going down like that.

A flapping noise reached my ears, and turning my head, I caught sight of the gray under feathers of a turkey flailing about. Turning, I struck out towards it, but that took me straight into a thick bramble patch. The gripping thorns ripped and tore at my shirt and bare flesh, leaving countless tiny gouges in my skin.

When a rabbit chomped down on my calf, I realized my tactical error. Briars do a real good job of tangling up big things, like clumsy humans. Small creatures, however, could just bebop close to the ground and run right under most of that mess. I had no doubt there were a dozen or more small critter-sized trails through this bramble patch.

None of that was really on the forefront of my mind at just that second, however. Instead, my focus was on the fucking rabbit with its pointy little front teeth trying to tear a chunk out of my leg. I kicked out, hoping to have similar results to my first kick, but this rabbit was much fatter than the squirrel, and when I kicked, I kicked right into the briars. I shook the rabbit loose, but in turn ripped my leg right up with thorns.

Spinning, I flung the fire orb and it hit the bunny with a glancing blow. Being magic, however, that was all it took, and in spite of the rain, the blood-thirsty critter went up in an instant. Magical fire doesn't fuck around.

The fire quickly spread to the surrounding briars, blue flames catching the thorny boughs alight. The magic spent itself quickly, however, and within a heartbeat, all that was left was mundane fire, which the wet and rain smothered. Regardless, I was already on the move, trying to rip through the last of the bushes before anything else could attack me.

I broke free, and as I ran, I summoned up yet another ball of fire. I could feel the drain on my system, not enough yet to be really worrisome, but enough to remind me that my power, even drug-fueled, was far from unlimited. Once summoned, I glanced back behind me, holding the orb aloft. What I saw caused me to stop.

Peering out from the edge of the briars were dozens of sets of eyes. They were reflecting the flame of my magic, and dozens of smaller blue orbs were peering back at me. They weren't moving, having stopped at the spot where the ground began to clear.

Over my pounding heart, the wheezes of my breath, and the storm, I heard a sound that instantly caused me to freeze in place.

Wind chimes.

And if they were close enough for me to hear them in this storm, then they were far, far too close. Turning slowly, I raised my eyes, looking around for the chimes. I fed a bit more power into the flaming sphere, to both increase the light and to prepare. Just in case.

I spotted a set of the chimes a dozen yards away. Made of bamboo we'd cut from the backside of the property, they were old and heavily weathered. Thick cords of twine held them to the limb above, and as the wind blew, they twirled and slammed into each other. Their hollow clanking echoed bleakly through the trees.

There was no way to tell what the Pooka had done to the minds of the rodents to get them to attack me. Maybe it had made me out to be a predator after their offspring, or an extra tasty nut. But whatever it had done, it wasn't enough to get them to enter the area around the witch house. I didn't blame them. I certainly didn't want to be there.

Sliding over to beside an oak tree, I carefully leaned against it. I couldn't decide whether to snuff out the light, or keep it around for protection. It certainly drew the eye, but then it took a few seconds to summon up. A few seconds could be all the difference.

The storm was still raging, but it seemed to be relenting ever so slightly. The clanking of the chimes was not as frantic, and there in the lee of the tree I wasn't actively getting more soaked. Though to be fair I had already reached maximum wetness, I figured. Glancing back to the briar patch, I saw fewer eyes looking back at me.

Whatever magic the Pooka had woven was weakening, I figured. The creatures were fading away into the forest, and the storm was going back to normal. That meant it was focused on something more important than trying to keep me from catching it.

A shriek tore through the night, inhuman and horrible. It seemed to be coming from all directions, carrying on the swirling eddies of the wind. It was a cry of pain and terror, and it chilled me to the bone, raising the hairs on the back of my neck.

I snuffed my orb right the fuck out. I wanted no part of whatever that was, and decided that discretion was the better part of valor. The Pooka was out there, and even though I needed to get it gathered back up, being dead wouldn't help matters none.

The darkness was terrifying. With the storm blocking whatever moonlight there would have been, it was inky black there in those woods. I listened hard, but after that one scream, all I could hear was wind and chimes. I took to peaking around the tree to either side, trying to get some sort of feel for what might be happening.

Lightning cracked, sending electric blue light to split the darkness. As the light faded, I caught a glimpse of bone-white. It was a split second, just short enough to leave me doubting that I actually saw anything, that maybe it was just an echo of light on my eyes. I knew better though.

The bark of the oak I was clinging to was digging painfully into my skin, so tightly was I holding on. If I could have melded into that wood, I'd have done it. Instead, I carefully glanced around, looking for signs of the Pooka. It was so dark that I couldn't see more than a score of feet away.

Lightning scarred the night sky once again, a long forking blast that struck so close that the thunder was almost deafening. In those scant seconds though, I found what I was looking for, and regretted that I had.

The reanimated turkey was dragging itself across the ground, flopping horribly on broken bones. Its one remaining wing flapped weakly as though it was trying to take flight, but was failing miserably. Its head hung limply on a broken neck, bobbing with every shuddering motion of the corpse.

Several feet behind it lumbered a rough amalgam of bones in the shape of a man. The bones were clearly not human, being hodge-podge of varying animal bones and capped with a black painted cow skull. Its long horns looped outwards, ending in golden points.

Silently, it stalked forward, raising a boney fist. The fingers of its hand were more like sharpened spikes than actual digits, and even curled inward, it looked lethal. Then the light faded and I was left in the dark once more.

I heard a meaty thwack, like someone tenderizing a steak. It was loud enough to be heard over the tail end of the thunder, which left me feeling sick to my stomach. I had no idea what effect a blow like that would have on the Pooka, but I suspected it was now having an even worse night than I had been.

White light split the sky and I could see the figure in bones had gripped the corpse of the turkey by its wing, and with one spinning twirl, sent it hurling through the night. The carcass sailed over the brambles, out of my line of sight. The creature was already turning though, not bothering to watch.

As the darkness fell once more, I kept my body as still as possible. I knew in spite of the lack of eyes in that skull, sight was no problem for the monster. I hoped he thought that he'd successfully driven the interloper from his home turf, and would go back to doing whatever it was that soul-bound piles of animal bones did at night. So long as it let me be.

I heard its heavy footsteps coming closer. It wasn't running, or moving especially quick, but at a steady pace that contrasted with the quick pace of my heartbeats. Each lumbering step brought it closer to me, and as silently as possible I got ready to cast a spell. It wasn't until the damn thing had passed by that I realized I had been holding my breath. I let it out as slowly and quietly as I could, in case it was closer than I thought. Then I slipped from behind the tree and in a crouchy, scuttly run took off for the briar patch.

I didn't dare light up another ball of flame, so it was slow, delicate going when I reached the brambles. Not being pursued, at least none that I was aware of, I was better able to navigate the thorny mess, only getting a few more small cuts to add to my collection.

The Pooka was lying there unmoving. I wasn't sure if it was sort of knocked out, or if the body of the turkey had finally taken enough damage to become immobile. Either was just fine with me, I thought, as I crouched down beside it.

Pulling out the empty butter tub, I popped off the lid and set it beside the carcass. "I shoulda done this from the word go," I muttered, cracking my fingers in anticipation. "But you can never tell how Granny might react to somethin' and I figured it would be best to return you the way I found you. But you changed the game now."

Putting a hand on the head of the turkey, trying my best to ignore the blood that covered it, I started muttering a few words. I no more knew what they meant than you would, but I knew what they would do: pull that Pooka up out that turkey.

A faint golden glow began to spread under my hand as the spirit entered my grip. It felt cold and slimy-like, as most trickster types do, but the fact that it wasn't fighting me or trying to wiggle loose told me it was solidly dazed. With it in a firm grip, I slammed it into the tub and slipped on the lid.

I took a little of the blood on my hand and etched my sigil on top of it. With a few more words, and a little more wiggles, that tub was sealed up in such a way that only me, or someone a lot more powerful than I was could open it.

All that had taken a good bit out of me, and with the rain still pounding down, I staggered to my feet and started the walk back to the van.

20. Special Delivery

It was maybe an hour before dawn by the time I made my way up the dirt road to my family's houses. The rain had subsided, thankfully, having drizzled to a stop an hour earlier. My thighs however were so chafed that every step caused me to flinch in pain as my jean shorts rubbed against my skin.

Coupled with dozens of rather nasty cuts from my run through the briars, it made walking a pain. It didn't help that I was crashing hard from the drugs, leaving me feeling strung out and weak. I either needed to do more, or get some sleep. I was pretty sure how I would decide.

I could feel the Pooka stirring in the tub I held under my arm. It was drifting around in there, testing the limits, seeing if it could weasel its way out. At least that's what I figured. Who knew what it was really doing.

It had made my life hell last night, but easy come, easy go. Being honest with myself, I felt sorry for the damn thing. It would be going back in Granny's basement until such time as she found another use for it. Which knowing her wouldn't be at all pleasant.

Grimacing, I squatted down and sat the tub in the mud. Reaching into my pocket, I pulled out a handful of old, ruined blackberries. They were dried-out husks mostly, turned rock hard with age. I'd had to go a little out of my way to snag them, but one thing about Jubal County, is there is no shortage of thorn bushes.

I tapped the lid, sending tiny little jolts of power in. "Now you behave yourself, I got a treat for you."

Carefully, I cracked the lid just enough to slip the berries in one at a time. There was no doubt in my mind that the damn thing made a move to bolt out, as I was sure I felt the container rock a bit. But the moment that first old berry fell in, the Pooka settled down. It might have been a shock, for all I know.

Everything had gone to shit. I hurt pretty bad, I felt like ass, and the van was all sorts of wrecked. But doing that one little thing, that didn't really cost me anything but five minutes of time, well, it made me feel pretty good. Like I'd done just the tiniest little bit to get some good karma rolling my way. Straightening, I rolled my neck to try and work it loose. "Well, let's get this over with then."

The peeling white walls of Granny's home reflected the moonlight slightly, giving the place a spectral feel. It loomed in front of me like a bulging ghost, waiting to swallow me whole. I wouldn't be the first to disappear after visiting family, legend held.

It was late, or early, but I felt eyes on me. There was no reason to think that Granny was waiting for me, expecting me, but I had a sinking feeling that she was peering out one of the dozen windows, watching me approach. A small lamp was on in the parlor, I could see it faintly through the rotting curtains that covered the window. It cast a dingy orange square of light, and I thought I caught a glimpse of a shadow moving.

The yard gate screeched as I opened it, and again as I pulled it closed behind me. The yard was overgrown, with weeds growing up to knee height in most places. It was thick enough that I had a hard time finding the stepping stones, so I ended up just traipsing along without looking.

My heart pounded as I set foot onto the first step. The grey, weathered board creaked beneath my boot, as did the next, and the next. The whole porch, like the rest of the house, had seen better days, and in places nails jutted up as they worked their way out of the boards they'd been driven in. More than once over the years I'd tripped over one, catching a shoelace or bit of jeans on them.

I stopped, my gaze falling on the small object before the door. I could see it was an old mason jar, its lid rusty with age. Inside was a slip or two of paper, with some kind of liquid in the bottom. It was a spell jar. My eyes went from it to the windows and back again. It seemed Granny had been expecting me, and had me a readymade receptacle for her little Pooka pal. All I had to do was pop it in there for her.

I don't know why it made me as angry as it did, but I was pure boiling with spite in a heartbeat. If that old hag wanted me to do her every little bidding, the least she could do was have the decency to tell me to my face. After the night I'd had, I was owed that fucking much, I knew that.

With a snarl, I tossed the tub down on the porch beside the jar. She had the power to break it open, and I would be damned if I would make it easy for her. I spat, then turned and stalked off through the yard, heading for the yard gate once again.

I swear, from behind me, I heard a cackle.

21. Interior Design

When the red glow of the taillights had rounded the corner, I finally walked over to my shed and after unlocking it, rolled it open. It was hard to tell if it was just how I had left it, considering how generally junked up it was, but at a glance I figured it was. Stepping inside, I set my box of oblivion, recovered from the van on my broken recliner.

Pulling the string, I turned on the light and carried my prize to the back of the shed. I'd kept the totem, figuring it would look mighty fine hung up on my wall. Nice and creepy, and generally fitting in with the ambience I tried to keep up.

"I see you made it back okay," came a voice from the door.

I glanced back, recognizing the voice. "I did. Thanks for closing up the shed for me."

The man shrugged. "Anytime, you know that." He nodded to the deer skull in my hand. "Go hunting?"

I snorted. "Something like that. Figured it'd look good hanging up here." I sat the skull on the bed then started rummaging around for a hammer and nail. With as much junk as I had inside here, there was a safe bet I had almost anything useful. Finding it was the hard part.

"Was that your Uncle Mike I saw pulling out of here?" Corey asked, settling on the edge a stack of totes.

"It was." Mike is my least favorite uncle by far. "H.D., he's uh...he's a little mad at me at the moment."

That actually had me worried. I'd gotten H.D. riled up a time or two over the years, sure. Hell, there wasn't a body alive who'd spent more than five minutes with me who I hadn't like as not. But I'd never seen Hubert Dale react like this. When he saw the state of his van, he looked at me one time, then without saying a word, he just turned and stalked off back in the house. You could feel the anger coming off him in cold waves.

That's when Mike had offered to run me home. And proceeded to lecture me at length as he always did, the only variation on his usual sermon being about how you had to worry when H.D. got quiet angry like that .

At this point in my life, I really only had two folks that I would truly call a friend, and he was one of them. I'd be lying if it didn't worry me, him acting that way. All there was to do though was give the man some space, I reckoned.

In the meantime, I had found a hammer and a screw. It would have to do for now. It took some pounding, but with a few hard blows, I had the screw buried deep enough through the plywood that lined the walls of these sheds to hold up the skull.

Stepping back, I admired my work. It was a little off-center, but it was too late to do anything about that now. But the way the charms and crystals and such hung down from the antlers, I knew when I had the fan going, and they'd look right pretty swaying around. With all that black and gold paint, I was of half a mind to see if I could track down some black spray paint, do up the whole back wall. But that sounded suspiciously like work, and I was crashing hard. Corey had been chatting at the back of my head, something about his divorce or some such bullshit. The man was really just giving me a sobstory in order to get him high. Which, to be fair, was a move I had pulled a number of times over the years. So who was I to really begrudge him, even if it did strike a nerve just then?

"I was thinking I'd smoke a joint, then get to bed." It was midmorning, but then I hadn't slept in a couple days at least. It was time. "Care to join me?"

Corey hemmed and hawwed, but in the end, of course he did.

I was dead asleep within ten minutes.

22.   Like Christmas Morning

When I woke up, it was dawn again. Using the power like that usually left me in a damn near-dead slumber, if I ever let myself sleep. This was one of those times, and I could already tell I was going to have a wicked headache from too much sleep.

Forcing that busted recliner into a more upright position, I spotted something unusual. There, on top of my stack of totes, was a golden cup. Rising to my feet, I walked over, stretching deeply as I did so.

It was small, about like a coffee cup really, but gold-colored. It might have actually been gold for all I could tell at that moment. Looking inside, I could see dark liquid, like some sort of red wine. Without being touched, it swirled gently inside, spinning in a gentle spiral.

Fairy stuff.

Leaning in, I took a deep sniff.

Blackberries.

I smiled. Someone, or something was happy with how I treated that Pooka. Odds were, it wasn't even poison. And if my history with fairy folk had taught me anything, it was that their liquor was rarely just that. Without a second thought, I downed the drink.

It was sweet on my tongue, and the flavors swirled and eddied all through my body. Smiling like a possum eating briars, I fell back into my chair and waited for the high - or the poison - to set in. It was a win/win either way, I figured.

And if I lived, that cup might be worth pawning, I reckoned.

Dancing With Your Demons

Being the second tale in the Redemption of Howard Marsh.

1. It's Not So Much The Heat...   (Summer)

For what felt like the hundredth time, I slapped at the buzzing of a deer fly. I missed the damn thing by a good six inches, slapping my stomach instead with a wet 'thwack.' It was far too hot to even think about wearing a shirt, so my hand hit bare flesh that was soaked with sweat.

It was barely seven in the morning, but it was already hot enough to leave me feeling absolutely miserable. Add in the flies, which were damn near swarming me, and my temper was none too pleasant. I cursed myself a fool for ever leaving the comfort of my shed that morning.

Around me the city of Elk Grove was waking up. I was walking past the Hardees, the busiest restaurant in town on any given morning, and there was a line twenty cars deep in the drive through all trying to get their orders in. Otherwise all there was of note were a half dozen other buildings that had seen better days. That was Elk Grove to a T: a place that had seen better days, and showed it.

I glanced down at the bag I was carrying though, and decided that it had probably been worth the trouble. It was an old messenger bag with a broken shoulder strap, and at that moment it was filled to overflowing with all manner of treasure. The kind worth rousing myself up outta my shed for.

Folks would leave all manner of goodies on the porch behind the Christian Mission, donations of things they didn't want or need anymore. I'd learned years ago that if you got down there early enough, before the employees would show up, you could get first pick, and as a bonus not even have to go to the trouble of trying to shoplift it from inside, or worse, actually pay for it.

Today I'd scored a few good shirts - not that I would be wearing them anytime soon - to augment my somewhat raggedy wardrobe. There had also been a box of books, so I had scored myself a few good reads; a John Grisham, a Glen Cook, and a couple of pulpy sci-fi novels. Good time wasters for when the heat of the day was in full bloom and it wasn't quite time for a nap yet.

There had been a stack of old vinyl that I would have loved to scoop up, but I didn't have a record player. I thought about maybe trying to get one, but I knew me, and figured they would sit in a stack somewhere in my shed gathering dust. Besides, I was pretty sure they'd just end up warped from the heat. It could get a good 100 degrees in there.

CDs though, there had been a small selection of them, and some tape cassettes. I had shit that would play both of them, so I had gathered up anything that even sorta caught my eye. Music was something of a passion of mine, even if I could no longer play an instrument, or carry a tune, than the man in the moon. But I was now richer by a few Genesis CDs and a rather eclectic mix of southern rock tapes. That would help pass the time.

Smacking my neck, my palm came with a smear of blood. I was too late on that one, and the stinging bite was already welting up I was sure. At least I had gotten the little bastard. One down, another thirty or so to go.

If I'd had the money I would have walked into the Hardees and gotten myself a biscuit and a cup of coffee. I hadn't slept a bit last night, and had no plans to do so anytime soon, so some nice dark coffee would have helped that process right along. But I had maybe fifty cents to my name, if that, and it would probably require digging through the cushion of my recliner to get.

Times were a little harder than normal if I was being honest with myself. I'd gotten fat paid from Rutherford last fall, enough that should have held me in good stead for months to come. But damned if I didn't end up using every red cent to fix my Uncle Hubert Dale's van. Sure it might have been my fault it took some of the damage, but hell, the damn thing hadn't even been worth three grand I'd have thought.

He still wasn't really talking to me much, though he was starting to slowly come around. Figuring I needed punishing I suppose, he hadn't visited me at my shed since it had all went down, whereas before I was used to seeing him at least once a week, if not more. It made for some lonelier than normal times, that was for sure.

Which, leave a body lonely too long, he's gonna get himself into trouble. Which I did a bit. Without much in the way of company, or a way to get around consistently, it ended up meaning I was spending more than usual on drugs to keep my mind occupied, but simultaneously earning less money. So now I was a good three months behind on shed rent, and really only had enough drugs for a couple more days.

I live low, but not typically this low. It was almost enough to make a body think about changing his ways.

Almost.

Last time I had been out that way H.D. had actually stopped and talked to me though. So he was coming around. I just had to be patient, and things would go back to their usual state of normal. Which for me was not typically really very normal at all, but it was what I was used to.

I was so lost in my pity party that I hadn't heard the truck coming up behind me. It wasn't until it honked, and I shouted like someone who just caught the holy spirit, that I realized I wasn't alone.

2. Water You Doing?

Heart pounding fit to bust I turned and saw the source of the honk. It was a small, two door truck, what looked to be an s10 or something similar. It was that kind of green that made you think of the ocean - not the forest - though the paint job was flaking in a few spots, with a bit of rust showing in places. There was nary a dent on it however, which was somewhat of an oddity in Jubal County.

"Sorry about that," said the young man sitting there behind the wheel. He was leaning against the open window frame, his hat kicked way back on his head. "I hollered atcha, but I don't reckon you heard me."

I was more pissed that he saw me get spooked than the fact that he had spooked me. "Well you got my attention now," I snapped, angrier than I had intended. "Can I help you?"

The youth, who looked to be about sixteen grinned broadly, his lip fat with some sort of dip. "You're Howard Marsh aintcha?"

I frowned. I certainly didn't recognize this youngun, but that didn't mean he wouldn't know me. I have a certain notoriety in these parts I suppose. "Depends on who's asking."

The boy spat a dark stream of phlegm from his mouth, which landed on the asphalt with a little hiss. "I'm Anthony Forrest, Inez Richmond's boy. You was..."

"You're Thomas's little brother?" I asked, looking closer. He did look sort of familiar, though with the mangy stubble of a beard the boy was trying to grow it was hard to tell.

Looking uncomfortable Anthony shifted uneasily in his seat. "Yeah," he said.

Thomas Richmond was in prison for burning down a church. A church with a bunch of folks in it at the time. A few of which it seemed happened to be federal agents. I could see why the boy wouldn't put that knowledge out there all willy nilly. He didn't know I was under the firm suspicion that there was more to that particular story than the government was letting on.

A deer fly bit my shoulder blade, and swearing I slapped at it. "Well we just chit chatting, or you stop me with a purpose?" I slapped fruitlessly at the swarming flies, none of which seemed to have any interest whatsoever in Anthony. "Cause I'd just as soon be up out this heat."

"My grandpa, he said you could water witch. That true?"

I nodded. "Yup, I've been known to find a pipe or two over the years. Learned it from my grandad."

The youth smiled broadly. "Well I got twenty bucks for ya, iffen you'll come by the house and dowse where some pipes are."

A pair of deer flies smacked me in the face, trying to land and thus feast on my blood. "Tell you what, I got time now if you'll just get me out these fucking flies."

3. Working Hard For The Money

The little truck didn't have working A/C, but with the windows down it made the heat rather tolerable. It was clean inside though, far cleaner than I would have thought it would be. When I'd been the boy's age, any vehicle I ever rode in had a floorboard full of trash. Hell, even grown up, most of the cars did, which was a comfort.

Some sort of country music was playing over the speakers, but not being a country fan at all, I couldn't have told you who it was. It was all just noise to me, whiny redneck music. You know what happens when you play it backwards? You get your house back, your wife back, your truck back, and your dog back.

That was what H.D. always joked at least. That got me thinking about the man again, which threatened to send me back into my little fit of melancholy. I tried thinking about something else, anything else, but you know how that goes. Try and not think about a thing and that's all you can think about.

I was saved from myself by Anthony piping up. "So I got plans to put a garden in the back. But I need help finding some lines so's as I can do it right, and not have to spend half my check on hoses the dogs will just chew up."

"Sounds like a plan. You got any welding rods?" That was the easiest way I had learned to water witch. Every other way involved hunting through the woods to find the right kinda tree with the right kinda branch. Or, in a real pinch I could use a coat hanger, but I always got mixed results with them.

Anthony nodded over his shoulder. "I got a pair in the bed. Grandpa said you'd need 'em."

Grandpa would be Inez's father. I remembered him; he was old and ornery, the kind of guy who got up before dawn every day to start chores. I always thought it was a miserable way to live. What he had to think of Inez...or Thomas for that matter. I knew what he thought of me at least, he'd made that a lot clearer when he ran me off the property with a few blasts of rocksalt fired from his shotgun.

It's not my fault he had a watermelon patch that was fairly accessible from the road.

From the looks of things Anthony was taking after him, and not his mother. Not too surprising I reckoned. It's not like any man stayed in Inez's life long enough to actually be a parent to the kid he spawned off of her, so grandpappy was likely not doing most of the raising.

148

Soon enough we were rattling down a hard packed dirt road that led to the Richmond Farm. It was a pretty country, dark green forest split up by the odd cow pasture or peanut farm. That was Jubal county for you, some of the prettiest country a body could ever hope to see, the kind of place city folk would damn near kill each other to live in.

Only if you looked closer you could see the rot. I saw the shell of an old house, little more than a moss-covered brick chimney sprouting up out a pile of collapsed grey boards, and half-hidden in a stand of pines. A mile later was a house with its yard full of rusted out husks of cars, littered with broken kids' toys and piles of beer cans.

Jubal County: a nice place to live, if you got rid of all the people.

I smelled the farm before we even got to it. Elias Richmond had four chicken houses, long silver buildings he'd had built out of sight behind an old oak grove. The trees however did little to hide the stink of chicken shit: the acrid, earthy smell filling my nostrils. It didn't bother me, I'd done my fair share of working in chicken houses over the years, but it told me we were close.

We jostled past a well-maintained yard dominated by a white painted two story farmhouse. I didn't see anyone, but Anthony stuck his arm out the window and waved regardless. The yard in turn was surrounded by the typical array of outbuildings you'd expect on a farm, sheds and barns, all filled with tractors and lord knows what.

There, right by the road still, was the watermelon patch. It was too early in the year for the melons to be ripe, but the spreading green vines filled a fenced in patch about half an acre in size. I knew if I was to walk in there now, there'd likely be fist-sized orbs of green hanging heavy on each plant. It set my mouth to watering in anticipation.

The curving drive that led back to the chicken houses came next, a broad line of packed dirt that cut through the trees. The smell was stronger here, with no wind that I could see to help shift it away. I caught sight of the tiniest sliver of silver, a part of one of the football field length roofs, and then we were past.

Rounding a gentle curve in the road we came upon Inez's house where Anthony, for now, called home. It had been a good three years since I had been by to visit, if not longer, but it looked unchanged.

It was a small trailer, and old, but well kept. The yard had been cut recently, but whoever had done it hadn't bothered to do the weed-eating, so around the skirting of the home tall weeds still sprouted. To the side they'd built a rough awning, and it was under this that Anthony pulled his truck.

An old wooden barn hugged the tree line, its doors long missing. It was up in the loft of that place that Thomas and I had gone a few times to smoke dope, or share a pipe, on those rare occasions that his mother was actually home. She was an addict herself, but damn if she didn't freak out if she suspected her kids of using.

The wind blowing through the truck windows had allowed me, briefly, to forget just how hot it was. Stepping out quickly reminded me as the heat blanketed me, threatening to suck the life outta me. Even there in the shade of the carport, I could tell it was going to be miserably hot.

The boy had reached into the bed of the truck and pulled out the two welding rods, and walking around the truck he handed them to me. "It's over here I need you to check," he said, as he began walking into the backyard.

As he talked, explaining just what all he had planned as though I cared, I took those rods and began bending them. I guessed they were about three feet long, and had a dull grey tone to them. Each was a little smaller around than a pencil, so in a few moments I had the metal rods both shaped up into 'L' bends.

Taking one in each hand I looked up in time to see Anthony pointing. "So yeah, if you would just set off across the yard there and let me know where that power line is run."

I nodded and raised my hands in front of me, bending my arms at the elbow so they sat about even with my belly button. Each of the rods I held real loose by the shorter length of the L, in such a way that they could swing freely about, but wouldn't go tipping out of my hands. I gave it a second for them to steady, then set out walking real slowly across the yard.

Truth is, there ain't no magic to it, least not any that I can tell. You walk until the rods start to turn inwards, and once they have crossed, boom, you found the pipe, or the line, or whatever it was you were looking for. I was pretty sure anyone could do it.

But water witching was one of the few of my monetary sidelines that was even close to honest money, so I wasn't about to go spreading that knowledge around. Folks who knew, knew I was a water witch. Which earned me maybe a hundred bucks a year, if I was lucky. But I was certainly in no position to turn down any money at this point.

I'd made it maybe twenty good long steps when the rods began to drift inwards. Another step and they were good and crossed, and one more past that had them spreading back apart. I took a step back. "Here you go, something here."

The boy had a few of what looked to be tent stakes in his hand, and carefully he stuck one in the ground where I pointed. "Reckon you could go across a few more times, maybe different places? So's as I can see how it runs?"

"Sure," I said agreeably enough. Twenty bucks for maybe five minutes work, well that's good money, I don't care who you are. "So what's your mom think about this garden project?"

Forrest spat. "Like she'd care," he muttered. "I ain't seen her in days."

That sounded like Inez. She tried to do alright sometimes, but when she fell off the wagon, she fell hard. And from what I heard, it had been some time since she'd even been in the same vicinity as the wagon. "How long she been gone this time?"

"A week." There was a whole lot of bitterness in the boy's voice, and I didn't blame him. It reminded me of myself; I too had spent a lot of time growing up home alone.

I had narrowed in on another spot, pointing it out for the boy to mark. I reckoned he planned to run a string from stake to stake, so he'd know where to watch out. At least that's what I would have done.

"That's a long time for her to be gone, don't you think?" I asked. Inez wasn't a good mother by any stretch, but she at least tried, when the drugs let her. I'd never known her to be gone more than three, maybe four days at most. But then, it had been a few years, so who was I to know how bad up she was these days.

Anthony shrugged. "Yeah," he relented after a few moments. "She ain't stayed gone this long before."

"You gone looking for her?" I asked, moving to the next spot the youth had indicated for me to check.

The laugh the boy hacked out was a soiled, angry thing. "You think I got time to run all over this county to find her? Someone gotta keep my brother and sister fed, and it damn sure ain't her. Between working for Grandpa, and looking after them when do I got time for all that?"

"Yeah, I feel ya," I said. I ain't got many flaws, but a real soft spot for kids with shit parents is one of them. I felt a pang in my heart that I wasn't really used to feeling to be honest. It was sorta like watching the end of Ol Yeller.

"She ain't even called," the boy spat. He had his can of dip out now, Timberwolf, the cheap stuff, and was slapping it against his leg to pack it down. "And the real pisser?"

Here he stopped. I watched him with a side eye, not staring, just watching curiously. As I looked, I saw him suck his bottom teeth, and sorta close his eyes. He had that look like he wanted to cry almost, but he would be damned if he was going to do that in front of me. The words warred inside him, but he managed to fight them down so's they spilled out without dragging a bunch of tears along with them.

"Since Tom went to jail, she'd been doing better. Finally got some act right in her, for the most part. Told me she was going to that big revival when she left even. Was gonna try and get her some Jesus, help her make sense of the Tom thing." He shook his head ruefully. "Ain't seen her since. Fucking figures."

I felt a flicker around my chest, a sort of flutter. There was an urge building in me that I was desperately trying to fight down and tuck back where it belonged. I'd been done similar a time or twelve over the years, and I'd be lying if I said it didn't sting.

"That's why I am doing the garden. I think I can grow enough to help keep us fed pretty good, what with what

Grandpa pays me to help on the farm. Figure there ain't no point in planning on her coming back."

"Fuck me," I said under my breath, as something inside me shifted a little, just enough to let a crack in my heart spread wide and let out something long buried.

"What's that?" he asked, looking up from watching my witching.

"I said I'd find her for you," and I inwardly swore at the words as they slipped out my traitor of a mouth.

4. Patience Is Key

"I've been coming out here once't a week and cranking it up and driving it up the road and back. So it still runs, least it did on Monday," Anthony was saying.

He was getting into a roughly painted blue Pontiac that was parked inside the old barn. It had been Thomas's car the boy had said, and after the feds had got done searching it, they'd turned it loose to the family. It was to be my chariot for the day, as I went and found Inez.

The car cranked right up, causing the boy to grin broadly, pulling the skin of his lip tight across the dip that bulged his cheek out. "What I tell you," he shouted over the sound of the engine. He clambered back out and stepped aside, waving me in.

The interior had a musty, moldy smell to it, but who was I to complain. I held up the spare key the boy had handed me earlier. "Now you're sure this is the spare key to your momma's car?"

"For the last time, I'm sure. I promise you that's it." He was still grinning. "Thank you again Howard. Even if you don't find her, I appreciate you looking." Pulling out a battered brown wallet he slipped a twenty and a ten from inside. "Here's your pay for the witchin' and here's some gas money. I'd give you more, but..." He tipped the wallet so that I could see inside it. I swear a moth flew out, and there were cobwebs inside.

Part of me thought I should probably give him back the ten, but then the rest of my brain told that goody-goody part to go suck a dick. I wasn't running a charity here, and I damn sure couldn't afford to spend part of the twenty I'd earned putting gas in this old hunk of junk. That was just the way it had to be.

Folding the money in half I tucked it in the pocket of my shorts. "I got a couple good places to look, and I know where she used to hang out. I'll get her found, no worries."

He just nodded, and stepped back away from the car, giving me room to pull out. I slipped the car in drive, and slowly pressed the gas. The worn shocks on the car left it swaying a bit more than I was used to perhaps, enough to let me know I was gonna dread driving it up the dirt road, but it would have to do.

The A/C blew air that was fractionally cooler than the outside, so I let it blow. I kept the windows down as well though, so the wind could blow in and help cool things down. It would also help with that musty smell I hoped.

As I picked up speed, papers began to swirl on the floorboard and backseat. One threatened to flutter out the window, but I snagged it before it could. A quick glance showed it was agenda or some such shit for a church session. I'd known ol Tom had taken to religion there towards the end, which is why I hadn't spent no time with him of note, but judging from the number of similar looking papers fluttering around he must have been going every chance he got. I crumpled the sheet up and tossed it on the floorboard. I didn't bother trying to stop any other papers from flying out, and soon enough I was leaving a trail of them down the length of the dirt road, like drunken doves flapping to their death.

I was about to the end of the road when I carefully pulled over. I parked beneath an overhanging oak branch, keeping as deep to the shade as I could without going into the ditch. Getting stuck hadn't gone real well for me last time it had happened, and I damn sure wasn't looking to repeat that debacle. Especially as I suspected thirty odd bucks wouldn't be enough to fix fuck all if I wrecked this boat.

With the car stopped I took that spare key in my hand, looking it over real good. It was a Honda key, not some Walmart reproduction spare key. That was good, otherwise this likely wouldn't work. Closing my eyes, I began to use the fingers of one hand to rub that key, while my left hand did a bit of twirling. All the while I muttered a few words quiet enough that if by chance someone did walk up they wouldn't be able to hear me.

While everyone knew me as a druggy and a small-time thief, and I mean everyone, I was known for other things. Like amongst older folks, folks who remembered my grandaddy, they knew me to be a water witch. But my most productive claim to fame however was finding things. If witchin' earned me about a hundred a year, finding things could sometimes bring me five, ten times that in a year, depending on how lucky I was, and how unlucky everyone around me was. Which being Jubal County, luck was always in short supply.

There was a catch though, which sorta limited my appeal: I could only find inanimate objects, and they had to be connected to something else in some way. The thing I was best at finding was a lost earring. I'd probably found forty different ones over the years, everything from diamonds to cheap but sentimental numbers. They were easy, cause the damn things always came in pairs. But there were other things, like key rings, or wallets, just depending on what the folks still had.

I felt the magic flow from deep down in my, squirreling its way down my arm to get a taste of that key. In my minds' eye I could practically see it, squirming around like a glowing, banded snake, tongue just a flicking. It sampled the goods, then flowed right back into me, leaving me feeling just a little bit more empty than I had been before this. In that empty spot however, there began to grow this tugging feeling.

Opening my eyes, I set off once more. Only now, I was listening to that pulling feeling. All I had to do was follow it, and it would take me to Inez's car. God willing she would be located right around there, and then I could browbeat her into going home. Or not, but then I could at least tell Forrest where she was, so he could try and guilt her home.

Either way, I was making progress.

5. Pro...gress?

I still didn't have a license, that would take far more money and finagling than I could muster even if I'd had the damn cash to do it. So I kept it nice and slow, and kept my usage to a minimum. I stuck to a nice, tight rolled blunt, the thick clouds of smoke I let flow out the window like some sort of modern day steamship.

It might have been hot enough to melt the tits off a brass monkey, but it was also a damn fine day. With the windows down the heat was tolerable, and the weed was mellowing me out enough that I didn't mind what heat I did feel. It wasn't a perfect situation, but it would do.

There was hardly a cloud in the sky, and the trees were about as green as you could ask for. Driving along I saw fields filled with growing corn and peanuts, even soybeans and a little cotton. The odd flower provided a splash of color on the side of the road, as did the glimpse I caught of the bright purple car I saw sitting out in a field.

I was in a weird mood. On the one hand I felt mighty dumb volunteering to hunt down Inez. But, it did make me feel...good? It was too early to say. I had no doubt that I would end up regretting it, as I did any other time I did something for someone else. I decided to not think about it, to just take in the day and try to make the most of it.

The tug of course didn't take me straight down the road. It sorta pulled at me, and if I had tried to follow it directly I'd have run off the road. As I was trying to avoid that, I ended up just doing the best I could. I knew all these roads, so it would take a bit of roundabouting I was sure, but I would get there.

In Jubal County there isn't much in the way of entertainment. You pretty much just have to drive up to Montgomery to find anything interesting to do. There is no movie theater, no bowling alley, no waterpark. If you wanted something to do you had to hope that high school sports were in season, which I always hated, or find a hobby like hunting or fishing. Those like me, we ended up choosing drugs, alcohol, and riding dirt roads. So even though I hadn't had a car in years, my time as a late teen still held me in good stead.

It's not like the county had had the money to build any sort of new roads for as long as I could remember.

My route looked to be taking me roughly in the direction of Jackson Hollow. Glancing at the gas gauge, I saw it had a bit more than a quarter tank. I knew old cars, not in a mechanical sense, but in the 'how will it fuck with me' sense, so I decided to go ahead and put that ten in gas inside. Partly to remove the temptation of me spending it on something else, which, as I knew me, was a real risk. Mainly though because I never liked to trust old gas gauges. I'd been burned more than once in that regard.

Turning onto Jackson Hollow Road had me pulling in the wrong direction, but I ignored that tug in my chest for the moment. I'd get my gas, then I would give into it once more, letting it guide me to Inez's car. As the One Stop was only a couple miles up the road, it really wasn't much of a detour.

The store looked same as it always did, save for a sign on the lonely pump that let me know they had started making folks pre-pay. That had been a long time coming in my mind, and I wondered how bad they'd got burned before they put a stop to the way things had been. Nodding to the old man sitting outside on a stack of milk crates, I stepped into the blessed coolness of the store.

Jerry Jackson was behind the counter, looking half asleep. He was also rail thin, and had a bad color to his cheeks. When he heard the door chime though he roused himself up, forcing a smile as he saw me. "Howard, how are ya know?"

"Oh, you know how it is, same shit, different day," I grinned back at him and set the ten on the counter. "Lemme get ten in gas. And how about yourself?" I asked to be polite, even though I really didn't want to. Either he'd lie, or worse, tell me the truth.

"Oh, about the same I reckon," he replied. "Just watching things til Emma gets back. She had to run to Elk Grove, get a few groceries."

I nodded, watching him slowly punch the numbers on the register. The cancer had him bad, that was sure. Whatever treatments he was getting, they looked like either they weren't working worth a damn, or they were about as bad as the damn cancer. As he shut the drawer, closing away what had been about a third of my net worth, he looked up. "All good to go."

"Thanks now," I said, and made my way back outside before he could unnerve me further. I set the pump to running, not like it would take long, what with gas prices being what they were, and leaned against the car door. I ducked my head inside the open window, keeping it out of the sun. I need a pair of sunglasses, but had long since misplaced my last pair.

Looking in I saw half my blunt sitting in the passenger seat, resting on top of a big ol' floppy bible that I reckoned had belonged to Thomas. Had I been smarter I would have tucked that weed under something, in case someone came by, but dead as it looked to be around there, there was little risk of that.

Staring at that blunt, I kept thinking about how bad Jerry looked. Which kinda hurt, seeing as he and Emma actually treated me halfway decent. Beside me the pump clicked off, but I didn't move to holster the nozzle back. Instead I reached over and grabbed the weed up, cussing myself out as I did so.

Walking back inside, I turned and locked the door behind me.

"Howard, what are you..." Jerry started to say, worry lining his face. I saw there a glimpse, just a quick one, that let me know that on some level ol' Jerry had always suspected this day would come. That it had just been a matter of time before I robbed the place.

I walked over to the counter, and slapped that blunt and my lighter on the table. "Jerry, we're gonna smoke this, so maybe you best crack that window there."

6. Valet Parking

The thing about Jubal County is nothing ever seems to be close to anything else. I swear I spent more time getting places, than actually spending time wherever it was I was aiming to be. It was enough to get on a bodies nerves, iffen you weren't riding a nice mellow high.

After smoking out the initially reluctant Jerry I'd boogied on out of there. Two good deeds in one day was wrecking the curve, but what was done was done. The good karma had already paid off however, as the gas station owner had given me a bag of chips and a pair of sunglasses by way of thanks.

Now I wasn't spending my day half blinded, and the once bright world had a faint grey tint to it, just like I preferred it. The chips weren't half bad either, hitting the spot just right with their sour cream and oniony goodness. The second best chips ever made I reckoned, behind sour cream and cheddar, which he unfortunately didn't seem to stock.

The tug in my chest was getting steadily stronger. The way the road curved for moments I would be headed straight for it, then I would round a corner, and I would feel it tugging from the right or left. But I was getting there, no doubt about it.

I finished the last of the chips, and wiping a greasy hand on my shorts, flung the bag on the floorboard. That lasted maybe a minute and a half before the thing got caught up in the wind and went hurling out the window. I wasn't much for littering, but then I also wasn't much for going out of my way to stop it.

The pull had me turning down a dirt road I'd never been down before. I wasn't entirely sure it wasn't an old logging road, as it had that deeply rutted look of roads heavy traveled by big rigs. With the busted shocks on the Pontiac, I was sure it would be a real smooth ride.

Within a half mile I was rattled about half to death as the boat I was captaining hit rough seas. I was lucky I had that weed in my stomach, keeping it nice and settled or I wasn't entirely sure I wouldn't have wound up hurling those chips right back up.

A mile up I found the source of the deep ruts: someone did live on this road, and they clearly drove a truck for a living. A tidy little double-wide was tucked back up a decently sized drive, alongside which was parked an old Peterbilt with a big rebel flag across the grill. I saw a skinny blonde woman on a riding mower cutting the grass, and she waved a thin arm in my direction as I passed.

Once I was past there the road smoothed out a fair bit. The tugging told me I was getting really close, and I was right on track. I knew I would be up on it at any moment, the way it felt, which left me to wonder what the hell Inez was doing over this way. It was not either of the two places I would have most likely expected her to be at, that was for sure.

When the tugging suddenly started pulling from behind me, I knew I'd passed it. I slammed on the brakes, and turning my head around I began backing up the road as carefully as I could. And then I saw it.

There was a narrow cut, something like an old driveway, that went up into the woods. Kudzu was thick on the ground, blanketing the area in its broad green leaves. And there in the middle of it was a Honda sized lump.

Parking the car I got out and looked into the green mass. Unlike a lot of folks I didn't have much of a problem with Kudzu. The damn stuff could have finished swallowing up the South any day now for all I cared. I just hated to have to walk in it. It had a nasty habit of hiding holes and snakes, and I wasn't too fond of walking into it either.

Looking around I scooped up a broken pine bough, and using it like a walking stick I began poking in front of me as I entered the vines. I tried not to think of what I was probably about to find. I had no desire to find an o.d.'d Inez. In this sort of heat, I could only imagine what state her body was going to be in. With each of my steps, I took to cursing her, her son, and the world in general.

The car had to have been there at least a few days. I knew kudzu could grow a foot a day, so it wouldn't have taken too long for it to cover the car like that, but it was still a matter of days. It would also make it a right bitch to look inside I reckoned.

Reaching the Honda I started tugging on vines, snatching backwards with more than a little grunting. It took a minute or two, but I got them peeled off of the doorway, enough so I could look in the window.

It was dark inside, the vines blocking a lot of the sunlight, but I could make out the interior well enough. The front two seats were empty of all but trash, that much I could easily tell. There was a lump in the back seat though, which I could only halfway see.

I stepped back, and sorta steeled myself up. This wouldn't be the first dead body I'd ever seen, but that wouldn't make it any easier. Reaching in my pocket I pulled out a couple of napkins I had grabbed from the car, and used them to keep me from leaving fingerprints. Taking a deep breath I ripped the door open, fighting the still clinging vines, and leaned over the driver side seat.

It was just a few blankets and a pillow.

I sunk into the seat with relief that there was no corpse. It was damn hot inside that car though, so I quickly got out, closing the door back. While I was glad I had not just stumbled upon the dead body of my old friend's mom, that meant my job wasn't done yet. I still had to find the woman. I looked around, wondering if her body might be lying somewhere nearby, under the blanketing kudzu.

Taking a deep breath told me that wasn't the case, as did the lack of buzzards. I could maybe try and spell up something just to make sure, but my gut was telling me she wasn't here. I'd learned to trust that feeling over the years, so I began walking back to the Pontiac.

"Well," I muttered, "guess it's off to Jimmy's then."

7. Jimmy's

My boy Jimmy was an eccentric, a genius, and a drug dealer all rolled up into one. In short we should have been best friends. We weren't quite on that level, but we were solid pals nonetheless. I think he kept his distance because he was always convinced I was gonna die soon.

He'd told me such a great number of times. Usually it came something along the lines of "Marsh, there's no fucking way you can...well fuck me. If you're gonna die, do it in the yard please." He had no great faith in my abilities, but I was one of the treasured few disciples so to speak that Jimmy allowed to hang around on occasion.

One of the others was Inez.

Jimmy kept away from any drug that wasn't weed or a hallucinogen. He was a masterful cook when it came to meth, the best in the county in my humble opinion, and a fair hand at producing or procuring any other drug you could think of. So while he never joined me in my forays into potentially more lethal drugs, he was rather fond of dropping acid with me. The conversations we'd get into, well I like to think that they'd have been life changing if we could ever remember them. That's what he kept me around for, his little LSD parrot.

Inez, I think he was in love with. At least a little bit. Jimmy wasn't the sort of guy to trade drugs for sex like some folks. But with Inez...well, I didn't get it, but I'd seen her get away with a lot of shit he never let anyone else get away with. Though I suspect you'd have to damn near torture the guy to get him to admit it.

Pulling into the junk-filled yard of Jimmy's place, it was pushing noon, and as I suspected I saw no signs of life. Our kind tend to be night owls, and unless I missed my guess, the man of the hour was probably not awake. I really hoped he had Inez in that bed with him, so I could go ahead and be about my business. Not that I really had any, but that wasn't the point.

I should have called ahead, but I hadn't had minutes on my phone in well over a month. That had been one of the first things to go. So I made a point of getting out slowly, and slamming the door as loud as I could. I even hollered out with a fake 'cacaw, cacaw' sound that was a sort of inside joke twixt the two of us. So he'd probably be ready for my knock in a moment, with a smile I hoped and not a pistol.

As it was I hadn't finished wading through the knee high weeds before the door to the camper opened wide.

Jimmy stood there in the doorway, hunched slightly and shielding his eyes against the sunlight. He had on a pair of plaid pajama pants and some sort of band shirt. "Marsh," he said by way of greeting, then ducked back inside the dim interior.

The steps up were as wobbly as ever, but I kept my balance with practiced skill, slipping inside where it was cool. I pulled the door shut, so as not to let out all the bought air, which left it dark inside. Jimmy flicked a switch and the lights came on in the tiny room that was both living room and kitchen.

The inside was old and worn, but tidy. Jimmy tried to keep things clean as best he could, which made my visits all the more fun in my eyes, the eternal battle between his cleanliness and my penchant for chaos. The man himself had slumped onto one of the bench seats that rounded the kitchen table, reaching for the remote to turn on the tiny TV that sat on the counter a few feet away.

"Damn son, you got any idea what time it is?" Jimmy sighed wearily. "Some of us work for a living, you know."

It was a joke as tired as Jimmy's voice sounded, and I let it just roll right off me. Instead, I slipped in across the table from him. "Good morning to you too sunshine," I grinned, trying to spread around a little misery.

The TV was on channel twelve now, showing the noonday news out of Montgomery. The volume was set too low to be more than indistinct noise, but that was something I'd learned about old Jimbo: he hated silence. Drove him up the wall. If he was awake, he wanted some kind of noise, no matter what.

"Didn't I just see you like, what, four days ago?" Jimmy was asking, his sleep-bleary eyes looking at the TV screen, not really seeing. "You ain't done everything already have you?"

I was low, but then twenty bucks wouldn't get me very far anyway. I decided to focus on the matter at hand instead of diverging into the land of acquisition. That could wait till after at least. "I'm looking for Inez. She been around?"

That woke Jimmy up, but judging from the look on his face, it woke him up on the wrong side of the bed. "Fuck no," he spat. "Not since...fuck, I don't know. Over a week."

I leaned back a bit. "What'd she do to get you all worked up like this?"

Jimmy huffed. "Last time I saw her, no shit, she did a rail off my junk. It was incredible. Then, nothing for days. No call, nothing. Then I hear from Jerm of all people that she's gone off and gotten herself some religion. Got 'saved' or some shit." The air quotes he threw around made his opinion on the matter pretty clear.

"So she ain't bought nothing from you in days?" Inez was never one to save; if she had five bucks, well, that was enough to get her going til the next bit of money came along. "That don't sound like her."

"Religion is the biggest blight on this whole damn county," Jimmy ranted. "It's just a money sink for gullible idiots who want to feel better about themselves. At least with my shit you pay money to actually get something in return, unlike praying to some invisible sky father that never did anyone a bit of fucking good."

"Tell me how you really feel," I said, grinning. I did mostly agree with him, however. Religion was a trap, a waste of money, and more importantly the religious folks in the area were dead set on fucking it up for the rest of us. If I had a dollar for every time I'd gone to buy beer on a Sunday, having forgotten that this backwards-ass county didn't do Sunday sales, then I wouldn't be in my current financial bind.

"First Inez, then fucking Jerm of all people. Two of my best customers, all dried up and gone away. I swear to god Marsh, you end up and get saved, I'll bash your skull in."

I laughed at the idea. "No worries there boss. I'm just trying to find Inez for her kids. She ain't been home in like a week or some shit."

Jimmy eyed me. "Mighty charitable of you."

I shrugged. "Moment of weakness, you know how it is."

"Yeah," the man sighed, slouching back into his seat, the anger deflated out of him. Reaching to the end of the table he slipped a cigar box from amongst a stack of them. Opening it, he glanced at the TV. "Want to have some breakfast with me, so's you didn't come out all this way for nothing?"

"I had some chips a bit ago but I could go for..." I started before a glance from Jimmy cut me off.

"Not what I meant," he said, pulling a blunt from the box and holding it up.

Grinning, I nodded. "Guess my appetite done perked right up."

He reached his hand out, and I went to grab the blunt. At the last second he pulled it back. "Just promise me something first will you?" He asked.

I felt my eyes narrowing. "What?"

"When you find Inez, will you tell her I miss her? I don't care if she got clean or not, I just want to see her."

"Sure. Want me to tell Jerm the same thing? Profess your love to him too while I'm at it?"

Jimmy rolled his eyes and tossed the blunt my way. "Fuck that guy. He'll come crawling back on his own, you wait and see."

I fished my lighter from my pocket. "And Inez won't?"

A morose, thoughtful look came across my friend's face. "I don't know. Here lately, she's been different, kindly trying to get her mind right I think. That shit with Tom, it did a number on her I think." He sighed again, a regular Eeyore all of sudden. "I mean I can't really blame her I guess."

I took a toke off the blunt, letting out a few coughs, then passed it back. We sat there in silence, smoking some of his best weed, each of us lost in our own thoughts. I was sure he was thinking about Inez. Me, I was thinking about how I kinda wished he had offered me some real breakfast. In my current state free food was right up my alley.

"Well," I said at last, breaking the silence, "I'm sure she'll turn up sooner or later."

8. Naptime

I woke up what must have been about two hours later. The TV was still muttering along indistinctly, making a muffled sort of drone that paired perfectly with the hum of the window unit air conditioner. Between those sounds and the weed, I'd done drifted right to sleep.

Straightening up I could feel that there was a bad crick in my neck now from the way my head had been lying against the seat. It was going to be a righteous bitch to work out it felt like, which did little to improve my mood. I was pissed that I had fallen asleep like that, and it just put more time between being done with this.

Sitting there on the table in front of me was a honeybun and a note which read 'Enjoy. Gone to work, good luck finding Inez." Peeling the wrapper from the pastry I wolfed it down, getting my fingers all sticky in the process. Standing up I began licking them clean, savoring every bit of sweetness.

For a moment I considered all the drugs there were in that stack of cigar boxes, and how easy it would be to help myself to them. The temptation was mighty strong, I'm not gonna lie. Jimmy would be back off in the woods, out in the little shed where he did his meth cooking, easily far enough away for me to grab and go without him being able to stop me.

I finally managed to pull my eyes off them boxes, and force myself to step outside. Robbing your drug dealer was never a good idea, especially when he happened to be one of your very few friends, even if y'all weren't exactly close. Not like H.D. Or my cousin Krista.

I shot one longing glance back at the camper, and the treasure trove it held within, then stomped through the weeds once more. With each step I got just a little more pissed at Inez. There was going to be hell to pay when I found her.

9. One Last Shot

On the one hand, I knew Jubal County had the most dirt roads in the state. So especially running in the circles I did, it only stood to reason that I would spend more than a little time on them. On the other, I was getting fucking sick of being all shook up because of the Pontiac's shit suspension.

I'd decided that I was going to check Yasmine's place, and if Inez wasn't there, then fuck her. It was getting on later in the day, and all I had to show for at this point after hours of work was twenty bucks, a bag of chips, and a damn honeybun. I could have been out scrapping, or trying to lay hands on some copper, or trying to score some yardwork. Much of my adult life has been spent wasting my days. But those were by choice. This was just pissing me off.

Yasmine's was literally the end of the road, which in a lot of ways was kinda a metaphor, considering what went on there.

The dirt road turned into a long driveway, lined with aged cedar trees. They grew so close together as to almost block the view of fields gone decades to waste, where once there had been a thriving farm. As the drive gradually curled up the low hill, Yasmine's came into view.

It was as stately an antebellum home as you could ever hope to see, all white paint and tall columns. Two stories tall, a dozen or more windows peered out of its front, most of them framed by neat green shutters and bathed in wispy white curtains.

In the tidy yard was a tall pecan tree, its spreading limbs covering the space in shadow. From some hung gaily painted wind chimes, from another was a tire swing idly shifting in the breeze. Flower beds dotted the yard almost at random, with small patches of riotous color that had clearly been well tended.

The woman of the hour was hunched over one of those beds just then, pulling weeds it looked like to me. As I pulled up Yasmine rose to her feet, taking off her gloves as she watched me pull up.

She was a tall woman, taller than me, her gray hair pulled back in a loose ponytail which allowed much of it to roam free. Errant strands curled around her face, framing a face lined with wrinkles. Thin, she had a dancer's grace still in spite of her age, and the overalls she wore were splotched with paint, but the white blouse she wore beneath them was clean.

Yasmine O'Connel had been away at college, for art of all things, when her parents had died in a car wreck. So she came back to run the family farm, only she had no more interest in that than I did. It showed as the farm slowly fell into ruin, and her attempts at being an art teacher didn't do much better, this being Jubal County.

The plantation home, which had been in the family since not long after the Civil War, was going to ruin. A weekly art class with maybe four or five students barely kept her fed, much less kept the old house up. She had grace, she had beauty, she had refinement.

More's the pity you can't eat that. Or pay your bills with it.

I'd never heard how it all came to be, but what I do know is her place became a refuge of sorts. Women on the run from drunken husbands, girlfriends hiding from stalker exes, and single moms with no other options. All were welcome to stay for a day or a week, till they got their feet under them, or at least an idea how to.

And for those who wanted to earn some money, well, Yasmine's became a whorehouse. That sort of open secret that the cops ignore, either because they are bought off with free pussy, or for those with some sort of a heart because she does a lot of good with her woman's home. That, or they

183

were just as afraid of the .38 that Yasmine always carried in case some asshole husband came around looking. The one she'd used more than once, and to good effect. Seems an artist's eye translated well to her aim.

I'd never visited as a client so to speak - if I had extra money it went to drugs, not sex. But when I'd been a kid I'd stayed here a time or two with my mother, hiding out from my dad. Yasmine had taught me to paint.

Turns out when you are a lesbian that runs a cathouse, the mothers of the community don't exactly rush to sign their kids up for your art classes anymore. So she scratched that itch by teaching the kids of the women who stayed with her. I'd had a little bit of skill she'd said, but like everything else really, that went the way of the dinosaur around high school.

"Mr. Marsh," she said, her face cracking into a smile as she saw me get out of the car. That was her way; everyone, no matter how down and out, how grimy and fucked up, they were always Mr. and Mrs. "It's been so long. You've done a lot of growing since I last saw you."

I nodded, and wished there for a second that maybe I looked a little less like the trash I was. Kinda like someone that art lessons might have stuck with, and less like someone who hadn't worn a shirt in three days, and hadn't showered in the past week. But that ship had sailed.

"Afternoon Ms. O'Connel. It's good seeing you again." I was surprised that I meant it, even as I was saying it. I hadn't had the best go of it as a kid, but the days I'd spent here had been good ones.

She reached out and put a hand on my shoulder, smiling warmly. "What brings you out my way? Come for a follow-up art lesson?"

I snorted at the idea of it, then grew serious. "I wish. But nah, I'm hunting Inez Richmond for her boys. They ain't seen her in a week, and I said I would help find her. I know she sometimes comes here when she's hard up for money, figured that might be the case now."

A worried frown crossed Yasmine's face. "Oh, those poor children. No, Inez isn't here, she hasn't been in some months in fact." She curled her finger and tapped it on her lip. "Do you think she's ok?"

I shrugged. "I found her car, but she wasn't there. I already looked everywhere else I could think likely. You were sorta my last hope."

Her frown deepened. "That's not good. I'll ask around for you of course. Business isn't on the up right now though, what with that revival getting everyone all worked up, but anyone who does stop in I will be sure to inquire. Do you have a number I can reach you on?"

"May be best to just call her daddy, Elias Richmond. My phone's out of, uh, commission at the moment."

"Of course, of course," she said. She looked back towards the house, then back at me. "I just wish there was more I could do. You're a good man Mr. Marsh, for doing this. Not many would take on this task I suspect."

I squirmed under her praise. "Well, I just had a little free time is all. You know how it is."

She nodded. "Can I invite you in for a glass of tea? I'm sorry, I should have asked earlier, I think the heat has gotten to my manners."

Shaking my head I thanked her for her offer. "I need to be getting on the road again I suppose. Miles to go before I sleep and all that."

"Of course," she smiled. "Come visit me sometime Mr. Marsh."

"So we can carry on with our lessons?" I laughed.

"Yes," she said, so matter of fact that it kinda took me aback there for a second. "I mean it. Come visit soon. You are too talented to let that skill lay idle, and we've wasted enough time as it is. I'm sure I have a few things around here that need doing and would most certainly pay you for, to make it worth your time."

"You're serious," I said, laughing again. I was a bit incredulous. No one ever pushed to spend time with me, ever.

"I expect to see you sometime next week Mr. Marsh," she said in a tone that brooked no debate. She was turning back to her gardening, pulling on her gloves once more. "And I'll keep an ear out for word about our dear Inez."

I stood there for a moment, staring at her, but clearly I had been dismissed. I was simultaneously annoyed and intensely flattered. With a nod I slipped back into the Pontiac and pulled away.

10.   Get Right

Seems like everywhere I'd been to mentioned this damn revival. And as the last place anyone seemed to have ever heard of her going anywhere, it was there. I'd been fighting that thought, as me and religion were no good buddies, but inevitability had its way of rearing its ugly head.

And if I was being really honest, I was doing anything I could to face the reality that the way her car was left, it said nothing good. She'd probably given the wrong trucker a rub and tug and was lying dead in a ditch somewhere. Or she'd taken a hotshot and was rotting in some abandoned crackhouse.

But so long as I kept looking, and not thinking about it, she was still alive and I didn't have to go back and tell Forrest something he didn't want to hear. So I decided that in spite of my general annoyance at the whole situation, I would make one last stop, just to see if anyone knew anything up there. Then one way or the other, I'd be done.

You'd have to be about blind to not know when and where the revival was. Even me, who typically lives with his finger terminally far from the pulse of happenings in the

County, had seen the flyers. Seemed they were stuck to just about every building in town, and in half the gas stations you could drive to in the area.

As it was, I knew that it was only about a twenty minute drive from Jasmine's, but seeing as the Pontiac's clock told me it was only a shade after four, and services didn't start on week nights until seven, I had a little time to kill.

Elk Grove wasn't exactly on the way, but I had time to spare so within a few minutes I found myself outside my shed, parking the car beside Corey's little blue Mazda. Even though his car was there, it looked as though he was gone, probably out having an early supper with his kids, or some such mess.

Didn't faze me much either way as I had tucked away the loot I acquired that morning. It took me aback there for a second how twisted the day had become from my original plan. Shrugging, I settled into my busted recliner and wished I had a beer or six.

That twenty was burning a hole in my pocket, and I had to fight the urge to spend it mighty hard. Which for me was rare, because usually I would just give into my first impulse. But I made myself a promise that I wouldn't spend it until after the revival meeting tonight, mostly because I suspected I would really need a beer then.

Instead I took to rummaging through my much depleted box of oblivion, weighing my options. What would have me humming along just right about the time I hit the sermon. Some of my favorite options were a bit too low I feared, so I ended up settling on a little something I'd been saving for a special occasion.

It's a hell of a way to pass some time.

11. Fucking While Camping Is In Tents

Royce Andrew was known for two things: being a god-fearing Christian, and owning what was probably the biggest cattle ranch in the County. He was the sort of man who would always make time for church, and revivals, and one who had enough land that he could spare a bit for a traveling preacher and his tent.

So it was that I found myself driving across his north pasture in a torrent of squeaking, screeching shocks, jostled about half to death. The grass was good and beat down, and even if I hadn't been following a few other cars and trucks, I'd have easily been able to find my way across the broad green expanse.

This time of year, the sun wouldn't be setting for another hour, but a few dark clouds were rolling in. It was looking like one of those late afternoon or evening thunderstorms you experienced around these parts for half the summer. They'd run real hot for a few minutes, coming on hard and heavy but would be gone quick as you please. A lot of noise, a good drenching, then moving on leaving the area even more humid than it was before.

The pasture was a low rolling hill, with the kind of worn terraces that you could tell meant this used to be some other sort of farmland, maybe corn. It made driving across it feel like a ship cresting waves, rising and falling all rhythmically. I was sure I was getting a lot more of that effect than most however.

Atop the hill spread a large canvas tent. It was a sort of tan, creamy color, in places almost light brown. It had probably been stark white when it's life began, but time had done made it a bit dingy. It looked well cared for though, without holes or noticeable patches, at least that I could see.

A double line of cars was forming up a hundred feet away from the tent, and I found my place at the end of the line, next to a shiny new F-150 with a pair of wrinkled old people inside who looked as if they were having some sort of heated debate. Why old folks wasted time squabbling I couldn't figure out, time was too short as it was.

I stepped out of the car, and I could feel the storm in the air. That sort of cool, crisp wind with just a hint of something electric in it. It was driving away the heat, making it feel about as nice as a body could hope for. Coupled with the excess exuberance the drugs had left in my system, I was in a far better mindset than I had expected I would be upon arrival.

A few folks shot looks in my direction, most of them none too pleased, but I didn't know why. I'd actually bothered to put on a shirt for the occasion, and one of my nicer ones at that. It was a Natural Light shirt I'd only ever worn once before, something I'd won or stole from a gas station in Sumpville. I couldn't quite remember at just that moment.

I couldn't be troubled to care much at all, feeling as good as I did. I started looking around as I walked towards the tent, looking for people I might know. Or rather, people that might be seen talking to me in public. I knew almost all of these people, and had done little odd jobs for a good number of them. But the sort of glances they cut me were all filled with daggers and darts and darkness, cut from the same cloth as the coming storm.

Fuck 'em.

I could see a camper with a little enclosed trailer parked back behind the tent, and I guessed that was where the preacher lived. The Reverend Silas Hatty the flyers had proclaimed, who was coming to save the poor sinners of Jubal County from the devil himself. I wondered if I counted more in the sinner column, or the devil column, and the thought sent me giggling, which earned me a few more looks.

The tent had rows of metal folding chairs underneath it, maybe a hundred, maybe a little more. I coulda done the math, but to hell with that. It was a good number, and even with the weather looking like it was about to turn to bullshit, it was a touch over half-full. Everyone was clustering around the middle of the tent however, away from the edges.

I prefer bad weather to most people, so I took a seat in the very back. I didn't much care if I caught a little rain on my shoulders, I could probably use a bath anyways. Besides, the way the storm was blowing in, I figured I would be mostly okay. Unless lightning struck the tent, then I reckoned we would all be dead. Which of all the ways to go, wasn't on the top of my list, but the irony of me dying in a church was enough to cause me to crack a smile.

"Marsh?" came an incredulous voice from behind me, one I knew pretty damn well, and was hoping to hear. I didn't even bother turning, aiming to come across as all cool and shit.

"Evening Jerm," I said, cool as you please.

12. Nice Shirt

I didn't have to look, I knew that I would see what was basically a taller, uglier version of myself. Pushing six feet and rail thin, with a number of prison style tattoos, maybe a few done by some kitchen scratcher; nothing that you'd pay real money for, cause let's be honest, real money went to drugs.

Jerm took a chair on my row, but two down from me, and leaned over stretching out his arm to shake my hand. I took it, fighting the urge to grimace as his clammy skin touched mine. "I'd have never thought I would see you here," he said. "Me here is odd enough, but you..." he laughed nervously.

"Maybe I wanted to see what all the fuss was about. Nice clothes by the way," I offered.

They were pretty nice, at least for such as us. A pair of khaki cargo pants without a stain on them, and a pretty nice long sleeved shirt. I mean it was clearly some sort of cheap Walmart one, and the colors were pretty faded with age and washing, but it looked clean. It'd once been dark blue with a purple stripe down each arm, but now it was more of a light blue, with a darker blue stripe.

"Had to dig deep to find these," he laughed. "Lucky my momma kept my old church clothes. And they still fit, more the shocker."

Of course they did, I thought to myself, seeing as he'd probably lost close to twenty pounds since high school. And it's not like he'd been anything but skinny then. Meth is a hell of a weight loss drug, if you discounted all the side effects. Though I guess teeth do weigh something. How do you think I keep my current svelte, girlish figure?

"Go figure," I said, trying to be polite. "Tell you why I'm here though, I'm looking for Inez. She got some folks missing her, and she ain't turned up in a while. I heard maybe she came here. You see her?"

"Fuck yeah I did!" Jerm said, then slapped a hand over his mouth. "I mean, hel...heck yeah I did. It was crazy man." He sat there shaking his head, a sort of wild look in his eye. Just shaking, not speaking.

"Well?" I prompted.

That seemed to knock the words loose. "See, it's like this. Both of us, we got to talkin' about how maybe things weren't going exactly how we'd always planned. You know how it goes."

I did, and I hated it. There was nothing more annoying than sitting around having a pity party with a bunch of downers. Not that I hadn't partaken of a few in my earlier days, but by now, my thought was either come to terms with it, or shut the fuck up.

"She said that Tom, he'd gotten his shit straight, well at least until..." he paused, thinking about all those people burning up in that church no doubt, "but it got her thinking that maybe she should do the same. And I don't know, it sounded good I guess. So we agreed to ride out one night, get us some salvation."

"Y'all ride together?"

"Nah, she drove herself. Me I got John and Dempsey to drop me off." Those two were his main running buddies, and no stranger to me, or Jimmy.

I snorted. "I bet they got a good laugh outta that."

Jerm frowned. "A bit yeah. But they did it anyway. I couldn't convince them to stay though. But anyways I was already there when she showed up, sitting about right around here. It was standing room only by the time she made it though, but wouldn't you know it, the Reverend, he'd saved her a seat special. Said he'd been expecting her a long time. Right up there by the front."

That didn't sit well with me at all. "Why'd he do a thing like that?"

Jerm shrugged. "I ain't heard it from his mouth, but I've heard folks saying it was an act of forgiveness, charity-like. Showing that even though her boy done a bad thing, she was still welcome in the eyes of god."

I had the decency to turn my head before I rolled my eyes.

"So the sermon starts up, and come time for the call to the altar, she goes right up there. And the Reverend, he laid hands on her, right there in front of god and everybody. She started sweating and shaking, and he started whooping about driving all the poison from her veins. It was some sure enough crazy shit, I'll tell you that. I swear that was all the drugs just coming out of her, cleaning her up."

His eyes were wide like saucers as he said it, but I could detect there was a desire there. It was scary, but he wanted him a piece of that. Seeing how rough he was looking, I had my doubts anyone had laid hands on him, purgin' him clean.

"She just passed right out, and some of the men folk scooped her up and laid her out on a few seats to recover. She was still out when my ride showed up, so whatever happened, it did a number on her that's for sure."

"You didn't check on her?" I asked, already knowing the answer. To be fair, I probably wouldn't have either, but then I wouldn't have been at the place at all, least not for such a dumb reason.

"Naw," he said sheepishly. "But I mean she was at a church with a bunch of church folks, what could happen?"

This time I didn't bother trying to hide my eye-roll. "You seen her since?"

He frowned. "No. I saw her car here pretty late that night, when we was out riding roads that night, but not nothing since."

"You ain't seen her up here enjoying her new salvation and such?" I asked. "Figure you get a miracle pulled on you, you would probably pop back in at some point. Just be polite I'd think."

13. Omens

I ain't much of one for omens. Well, maybe I am sometimes, it comes and goes we'll say. But I had to say the entrance Silas Hatty made was nothing if not dramatic.

Jerm was filling my ear with a bunch of jargon I didn't care about, but I did gather that attendance was down pretty dramatically that night. The way he was talking, it'd been standing room only pretty much every night he'd been, but I could see that close to half the seats were still empty. It warmed my heart to know that all those faith-loving people were scared off by a little rain.

The crowd though got real quiet of a sudden, and even Jerm shut up, when the door to the camper flung wide. Out stepped the Reverend in a stately calm, oversized bible in his hand. He began to stride purposefully across the pasture.

The storm was coming on now, all dark clouds and whipping wind. The air felt electric, and the wind was whipping the grass of the pasture like swirling waves. There was no rain, but you could tell it was coming at any moment. Hatty looked as though he didn't even notice the weather.

He wasn't real tall, but he was a solid looking guy, like a former body-builder. He was dressed in some grey dress pants under a plain white shirt with the sleeves rolled up above his elbows. His tie was solid black like his hair, but his face was clean shaven. All in all, he was an intense looking guy - no nonsense, no frills.

Striding into the tent like some sorta king of old, he made his way right up to the little podium that was erected there and slapped his bible onto it. Right then thunder rumbled ominously, rolling through the dark sky and, I am not gonna lie, giving me a little chill.

The man had dark eyes. In that moment they looked calm, almost warm, but they had the look of eyes that could go steel hard in a heartbeat. He made me think of every angry gym coach I'd ever had, all fun, games, and jokes until someone doesn't want to dress out, then the screaming starts.

He started in on the usual, opening with a long prayer that I swear must have taken five minutes. I didn't even pretend to bow my head, instead spending that time watching the crowd to see who cheated. Silas didn't. He kept his eyes tight and arms raised the whole time, really getting into it.

When that finally ended he started in on little bits of news, and prayer requests type shit. All of it didn't matter a fart in the wind to me, and I managed to tune most of it out. The only part that even kindly caught my attention, and only because of the gasps that accompanied it, was that he was gonna be closing up shop after Sunday.

"The work of the Lord calls me ever onwards brothers and sisters! There are many places yet filled with sin, so filled, that the churches there have forgotten how to act. Places that need that old-time religion!" he was saying. I was pretty sure that no place needed old-time religion, and just fought to stifle a yawn.

The rain started to fall, pattering heavily on the canvas of the tent. It came on in a sudden wave, not building from a slight sprinkle to the heavy pounding. With the wind blowing as it was, the rain was slanting under the tent, though no one was getting wet that I could see. If the tent hadn't had a canvas wall across the back, where Hatty was striding back and forth starting to crank up his sermon, I knew he'd have been about half drenched, maybe even the first row or two of folks.

He was the sort of fire and brimstone preacher you heard about, but never really saw anymore, which I personally thought was a blessing. Jubal County had lost most of its fire and brimstone types to actual fire when the

Church of Signs Revealed had burned down. But then, as Hatty had yet to start snake handling, I suspected that even he wasn't that bad.

That storm brought a cool wind with it that felt absolutely amazing, considering it felt like I hadn't been cool all day. This was even better than Jimmy's old window unit, damn near cold and with a dampness to it that was refreshing. I was half tempted to step out from under the tent, but I figured it wouldn't do to make too much of a scene. Least not yet.

He was really going now, whooping and hollering at the top of his lungs. He'd run across the tent, arms raised and bible flopping around. He rocked that podium back and forth so far you'd swear it was gonna tip over at any moment. He shouted, he cried, he roared. It was quite a sight, I had to admit.

About fifteen minutes into it though, a weirdness began to creep up my spine. I could feel more in the air than just that damp, crackling storm feeling. There was a sinuousness slipping around, oozing its way around the tent. There was magic in the air.

The human mind is built up in such a way that when confronted with magic, it will just ignore it. You have to be woken up to magic, have the right genes or something, before you can see it. But once you see it, it can much more easily see you, which is never a good thing as I have learned. But just because you are awake to it, doesn't mean you can just willy nilly identify every little thing about it.

There was magic in the air, but I hadn't a clue what it was doing, or who was behind it.

14. I See You Baby

I got an itch to go back to the car, to get away from whatever magical bullshit was swirling in the air. This whole situation had stunk from the word go, and the moment I found her car I shoulda just called the cops and called it a day. But for some dumb reason I decided to play hero, going against my gut, and here I was.

This whole situation was foul, and getting fouler. If there was magic involved, I wanted an extra level of nothing to do with this. The fact that she got 'saved' then disappeared said absolutely nothing good to me. My guess was she left here, went to find some old boyfriend and express how she'd changed her ways, and when she wouldn't give it up he'd done her in.

Only that didn't explain the magic, but maybe I would be lucky and those two things would have nothing to do with each other. Not sure why I thought that in this instance I would be lucky, but a boy can dream I reckon. All in all, I wanted back in the car, and away from all this.

Sadly, it was raining. And while I wasn't opposed to getting wet, unless something else began to happen I was fine where I was. At least until the storm broke. My hair was a bad enough mess without it sticking out every which way from a lightning strike. Though, maybe a good quick death would be my reward, which would be nice at that moment. Though knowing me, it would probably just leave me paralyzed, or blind, or something. I had enough going on without all that added on top.

On the other hand, if I got to the car, I could go into my box of oblivion and dig out a little something that would help me see things more clearly, both literally and figuratively. A little nibble on some 'shrooms, and maybe I would be able to actually see this magical bullshit without having to cast or do anything. Whatever it was, I wanted to stay off its radar as much as possible.

I couldn't see it, but I could feel it, lurking around the confines of the tent. It felt bulky and broad, like some sort of shuffling mass of blunt force. The way it was nudging around, it was almost like the...spell? creature? was nudging around looking for something. Like an old shaggy coon hound, too old to go chasing after anything, but still smelling around regardless.

It was pretty clear that if anyone else felt anything of the sort, they were playing it close to the vest. All eyes were locked on the Reverend, who was busy decrying the sins of the world in a booming voice, casting judgement on the

County. Though in my mind he was wasting his breath. If passing judgement on a thing actually made any difference, then I'd have judged this damned place out of existence years ago.

The creeping nothing found its way to where Jerm and I were sitting. The storm was really whipping now, and a few scattered drops were beginning to strike the back of my head and shoulders. Jerm swore a little under his breath and climbed between two of the chairs in front of him, moving to a dryer row.

I just froze in place, waiting for it to pass. It was a cold, burning thing, like holding onto a piece of ice for too long, consequently turning the skin a singed red. I swear I could hear the faint crackle of flame, like a distant fire, popping and roaring within this invisible nothing.

It washed over me, and I readied my hands to pop off a spell. I didn't call up the power, though I was on the very cusp. I wanted it to ignore me like it had every other person under that tent, to move on and finish what it was doing.

I felt like it was hovering all around me, taking in deep breaths of what and who I was. Feeling me out, gnawing at me just a bit to get a little taste of what I had going on. There was no actual feeling, not physically, but the mental impressions felt real in a way much of my life hadn't.

And then it passed. Was it all in my mind that it had lingered longer on me than anyone else? Or was just that drug fueled paranoia? Or my regular level of paranoia? I swear it seemed as though it was all over me for several minutes, five or six maybe. Before that it had just been threading up and down the rows, hadn't it?

It had moved on, and, which I guess was a good thing. I couldn't feel it anymore, though how an invisible thing can disappear, well that's sorta a mindbender in and of itself. Had it gone away because it had found what it was looking for? Or because I was just the last place it had set out to look, seeing as I was in the back of the tent?

Either way, I didn't like it. I'm not the lead expert of magical expertise in the County. Far, far, far from it in fact. But while I don't know much about what it is I do, I do tend to know everyone who can do what I do. And no one I knew was there in that tent that night.

There was someone doing magic, some kind I didn't rightly know, that was all cold and fire. Someone that I didn't know. And they were close by, and maybe looking for me, or folks like me. My eyes fell on Hatty, who at that moment just happened to glance my way, and our eyes locked.

15. Opportunity

Those eyes, they were like that spell, or whatever it is I had felt. An icy blue, much like mine, but there was a heat to them, that coupled with his ranting and raving came across as a mad intensity. They were only on me for a second, but they left me feeling some sorta way, that was for sure.

The rain was coming down a bit harder, enough to encourage me to get further under the tent. While part of me, the contrary part, made me want to stay, to not acknowledge my choice of seat might not have been the best, and I was tired of getting wet. I was also not real fond of the idea of getting closer to the Reverend after that rather hard glance of his.

In the end I relented, mostly because Hatty seemed to instantly lose all interest in me the moment he looked away. With a grunt I slouched down next to Jerm one row up, easing down so low in the chair that my head could rest on the back. It was metal, and a bit too hard for napping though, so that avenue was clearly out. I'd have to find some other way to pass the time.

A slap on my chest jarred me awake. I sat bolt upright, eyes wide, mouth open to go to cussing. I stopped when I saw Jerm with a finger across his lips, leaning real close.

"Jesus Marsh, you was starting to snore. Folks is staring," he whispered.

I looked around, and there were a few glares pointed in my direction. I didn't have enough shame to be embarrassed thankfully, so I settled back into my chair, though not quite as low this time. I could see Jerm eyeing me, making sure I didn't drift off back to sleep. That was fair, but I knew Jerm didn't have the best attention span.

The rain seemed to have mostly stopped, but it was full dark out now. The few lights that had been strung up in the tent cast everything in faint orange. What thunder I could hear sounded real distant, and no lightning struck as long as I watched .

I was mulling over ducking out the back, now that the storm had passed, making a tactical retreat before the sermon could end. I mean, I'd gone above and beyond, spending all damn day hunting after Inez. No one could blame me for calling it a day. Hell, I wouldn't be surprised if Forrest had called the cops and reported the car stolen at this point.

I had every right to leave...but I would be lying if I wasn't fucking curious. Where had she gone off to? Was she dead? Or just shacked up somewhere, maybe getting clean. Or cleaner, according to Jerm. There was one last person I could talk to, even though my gut was telling me to keep a wide berth.

Hatty. He'd have to know when she left if nothing else. And if I didn't follow up, it would nag at me. All I had to do was wait til the end, ask him real quick, then I'd be done and free to go home and drug it right up for the rest of the week, til the money and fun ran out. I'd more than earned it.

Besides, things looked to be wrapping up. Some old guy was walking from row to row with what I guessed was the collection plate. It was a dull grey platter, and I could hear the clink of change hit it. Those were outliers though, most folks were dropping bills inside. I'm not gonna lie, my eyes got sorta hungry watching that.

If the old man had an opinion on us poor sinners in the back row, he had the good grace to not show it on his face. Jerm had a wadded up dollar that he dropped in amongst the rest, then glanced my way. I smiled, in what I hoped was a serene, beneficent smile. Something befitting of Jesus.

I pulled my biggest bill out. "Can I get some change?" I whispered.

The old man nodded, a smile crinkling the wrinkles around his eyes. I made myself some change out of the plate, carefully scooping up a handful of bills. I quickly folded the twenty six dollars in half and tucked them into my pocket, before the man could realize what had happened. This stop was turning out to be more profitable than I had imagined. I might have to start going to church on occasion.

There was some more singing, and a good bit more praying after that, but the sermon drew to a close maybe ten minutes later. I let out a loose rattling sigh. I was oddly exhausted. Watching that man rant and rave could take it right out of ya.

Jerm stood first. "Marsh, you reckon you can run me home? I have to catch a ride tonight, Dempsey has work. I got," he fumbled in his pocket coming up with a small handful of change, "three bucks for gas if you can."

I thought about the six bucks I had just stolen. "Sure, for three bucks I can do that. Your place ain't too far from where I need to be." It was actually sort of on the way, but no way I was gonna tell him that. Then he'd want the ride for free, and the Howard Marsh Charity for Wayward Drug

Addicts was closing up shop for the night, and probably the rest of my given life.

"Great," he said, though smartly he didn't go ahead and hand me the money. Old habits die hard. "Lemme just say my goodbyes real quick, and I'll be good to go."

"No rush. I got some talking I need to do as well I reckon," I replied, eyeing Hatty from across the tent. He was shaking hands with a small cluster of people, all of whom seemed to be gushing about the sermon he'd just passed. Why was beyond me, but that wasn't for me to judge. Instead I hitched up my pants, metaphorically speaking, and strode over to make my acquaintance.

16. Face To Face

I ended up being at the back of the short line of people wanting to jawjack, which befuddled me. I mean, hadn't we all just heard this guy talk for the past hour and a half? What more needed to be said really? But I guess it was human nature; folks had to go suck up to the teacher after class, to show they understood the lesson. Even if the teacher was skipping town in a few days.

A few folks were asking him to stay longer, that much I did hear. One old woman who I didn't recognize, but from her looks reeked of old money, was trying to convince him to open a church, and she sounded like she was willing to help put up the money to at least rent a place. It was hard for her to get the point across, with that usual reticence of talking about money that those deep south old money people had, but I was pretty good at reading between the lines.

Hatty was an expert at deflection though, turning down all offers and requests without making it sound like he was. I bet half those people didn't even realize they were walking away with nothing. He was so smooth. He might be fire at the pulpit, but he was smooth butter away from it.

When it finally came my turn he reached out a massive ham of a hand. I didn't really want to shake it, knowing he was gonna be the type to try and pure crush me with a shake. I was surprised though, he shook firm, but not outrageously so. Not much I hate more than someone who thinks there is a straight line correlation between how hard you shake and how much of a man you are.

"I don't believe I've had the pleasure, Mr....?" He started.

"Most folks just call me Marsh."

"Well then Mr. Marsh, I want to welcome you to my service. Glad you decided to attend tonight, and I hope you took something from it," he smiled. It looked genuine enough.

I was struggling to get a read on him. Eyeing him up, he wasn't quite what I expected. For one, I had seen he was pretty stout, but up close I could see he was built like a brick shithouse. He was basically a walking talking muscle, and I had a suspicion that his camper was basically just floor to ceiling weights.

His shirt was tight across his chest, tight enough it was a wonder he hadn't split it in all his charades. So tight you could see the faint dark splotch of tattoos on his upper arms. The tail end of one actually poked out from the rolled up sleeve on his left arm. It might have been the bottom of an anchor, but it's not like I had all day to stare and puzzle shit out.

It was the eyes though that really drew me in. It was almost like looking into a mirror, so similar were they. I've always heard folks say 'I know it like the back of my hand.' I always thought this was a stupid phrase, because really, how much time do you spend studying your hand? I was certain I couldn't pick mine out of a lineup.

My eyes though, I'd stared in a mirror enough to know them. And eyes like mine didn't come along just any day. No one else in my family had them, not like this. You ever stand in a hall of mirrors, and stare off into one of those infinite regressions? I felt like if we locked eyes too hard, that same thing would happen.

"Well, if I'm being honest, I didn't come for the sermon," I said in order to distract myself from falling into those eyes.

"You come because these chairs make such good napping spots?" He asked with a wink.

I laughed politely at his joke. It wasn't right someone who preached so hard being so fucking likeable. "Well, that was a perk. But no, I came hunting Inez Richmond. I heard she was here."

Was there a flicker in those icy eyes?

"Sister Inez? She was here a few days ago, but I'm not really in the business of just spreading other folks' business around frivolously," he said softly. "Why are you looking for her?"

"Well her son was wondering where she got off to, asked me to look around a bit. Me and her, we run in similar circles."

His brow furrowed. "I thought her son was in prison."

I shook my head. "That's her oldest. She's got another few kids."

The furrows deepened. "Are they Richmonds too?"

That was an odd question I thought. I couldn't think why I shouldn't answer it, but I was getting less sure about where we stood. "No, they're from another daddy."

"I see," he nodded, a sad sort of look coming on his face. Was he worried about the kids? He seemed the type that would probably damn the mother to hell for having kids out of wedlock during service, but then would probably coach a little league team for them later that day. "Well I can tell you that she was here, and she experienced a cleansing miracle. She asked to be baptized, which I did right after the service. She left soon after. And sadly, she has not been back since."

He seemed genuinely upset by that fact. "And you say she has abandoned her children? Is there something I can do to help? I can't but feel responsible in some way."

Jubal County had gotten by just fine without folks coming from all over to try and save us, and we would do the same soon as they left. "Their grandfather is looking after them, it's fine. But you say she left right after? So what, like one, one thirty?"

He thought for a moment, then shook his head. "It was probably closer to two if I had to put a number on it. But I don't wear a watch." He raised his arms, showing his wrists were bare.

"Well, then the hunt continues I guess." I shrugged. "She'll probably turn up in a day or two, all strung out again. The word of the Lord can't compete with the high of the Meth I reckon," I chuckled.

At then Hatty's face grew hard. He reached out and shook my hand once more. "I do hope you come back Mr. Marsh. Do, and I will prove to you that nothing is more powerful than the word of the Lord."

He stalked off then, and I was left wondering why that felt like a threat.

17. Lies! All Lies!

Jerm looked to be about done talking, and I suspected that me walking up just then would probably do him no favors. So instead I just walked out of the tent, staying just inside the narrow band of light provided by the hanging lights. I pulled a cigarette from what was left of my pack and lit it. I wasn't alone in that at least, as there were a few others standing around smoking, waiting for their friends to get done talking.

There's a sort of camaraderie amongst smokers, especially these days when it gets so much hate. Those folks might have normally not given me the time of day, but one leathery old man actually gave me a slight nod, the warmest welcome I'd been given more or less. So I stood there and chewed things over in my mind.

There was no evidence to back it up, but my gut, it told me that Hatty was behind that spell. Or whatever it had been. If that was the case, then he was a lot more than he seemed. He wouldn't be the only preacher with a little power that I had ever encountered, but he would be the most devout. Someone who both preached, and could call down fire and brimstone? That wasn't a good combination. Not for anyone.

And if Inez was caught up in it...

The Richmond family was an old one around here. And while I'd never known one to get really caught up in the kind of doings I find myself in, there were some old, odd stories about them. Thomas Richmond burning down a church was almost par for the course when it came to that lot.

Jerm came walking up at last, asking to bum a cigarette. Very begrudgingly I handed him my next to last smoke. I supposed I would have Forrest run me by a gas station on the way home so I could buy another pack. I hated to spend the money, but at least it was one of my necessities.

We left the light, stepping into the night dark. The wet grass clung to my legs, and a few lonely drops fell on my head, the tail end of the storm still dripping from the sky above. Very faintly in the distance I heard a low rumble of thunder, but it was clear that the worst of the storm was over.

"Jerm?" Something was nagging at me.

"Yeah man?" He replied.

"You said Inez's car was here late that night, didn't you? Like after dark?"

He nodded vigorously. "Yeah, it was. I saw it from the road when we drove past that night. When we went riding. Dempsey and me."

"You saw the car, after dark, from the road, as y'all were driving past," I said blandly. The road was a good quarter mile away, and by the time you reached where the cars were parked, the light of the tent was good and faded. There was no fucking way. "That's your story?"

We had made it to the car by now. The dust of a day spent on dirt roads had only been partially washed off by the heavy rain. It had clung tenaciously to the sides, and now red-brown rivulets lined the sides, pooling in the edges and ridges.

Jerm turned to face me, his face nervous, but his tone defensive. "Yeah man, I mean what other story you think there is?"

I swung the driver side open and slid behind the wheel. Jerm mirrored me, and as I shut the door and turned the key, I looked over at him. "Jerm, you met my dad right?"

He shivered. "Black Tom? Yeah, one time. It was rough."

222

I looked him dead in the eyes. "He seem like the kind of guy to raise a fool?"

The other man looked down at his lap, then looked up and gazed around, his eyes drifting over the few cars still parked around. Most were getting ready to leave as well from the looks of things. "Look man, I'm just..."

"Jerm. Just tell me how you know. I don't need reasons or excuses. Trust me, I won't think any less of you." That was mostly because I doubted I could think any less of him. He was an alright guy to share a pipe with on occasion, but he had all the spine of a dishrag.

He sighed heavily. "We uh, we came up here to see if anyone had left their car behind. Figured it would be safe, you know."

"No cameras in a pasture," I nodded. "Guessing that was Dempsey's idea?"

"Don't matter really," Jerm said softly, and he was right. It didn't. "But yeah, her car was still sitting there, and it was the only one. I figured, well, maybe she'd have a little rock or two inside. And seeing as she wouldn't need 'em anymore, getting clean and all, she couldn't even be mad I took 'em. It was unlocked, but weren't nothing worth taking."

"Robbing a friend, that's pretty low," I said. I mean I'd done it, we'd all done it, but Jerm had sorta gotten on my nerves at this point so I wanted to dig into him a little.

"Oh fuck off Marsh," he swore. He glanced my way, and I could see tears were welling up in his eyes. "I just want what she got damn it. I been coming back every fucking service, and not once has that bastard laid hands on me."

He began to sob, wracking ugly snarls of tears that blended with snot and ran down his face. "I'm so fucking tired," he managed to gasp out. "I can't stop. I want to."

"But I can't."

18. Sometimes I Sits And Thinks

It was a silent ride. I didn't have anything to say, and it seemed Jerm wasn't really in a speaking mood. He cried gently into his arms for a while, then sat quietly staring out the window. I left the radio off, letting the silence wash over us.

Jerm didn't say a word until I pulled into the driveway of his mother's house, where he lived in a little outbuilding around back. He pulled the crumpled ones from his pocket, offering them to me. "Here you go," he muttered.

I glanced at the money, then sighed. "Eh, you're on the way. Keep it."

He looked at me, his eyes questioning, but I refused to look back. He shrugged and tucked the money away once more. "Thanks Marsh," he said, climbing out and then disappearing into the darkness behind the small, neat home.

I sat there for a moment, watching him walk away and debating on stepping out and asking for that money after all. It was half a pack of smokes after all, and I was soon to be tapped right out. Instead I put the car in reverse and carefully pulled out into the street.

A mile up was a small gas station, not some chain but a mom and pop number known as the Kountry Korner. It was closed, had been at least for an hour, but there was a pale white security light that lit the paved area which surrounded the pumps. It was there that I pulled over and parked.

I knew how Jerm felt. Anyone who lived like us, you got that way at some point or another. Usually sooner rather than later. It was a sort of world weariness that sapped the very life from your bones. Then you either got used to it, or it dragged you under.

I'd gotten used to it.

Jerm, it was dragging under.

I lit my last cigarette and thought it all over. Jerm had been treading downward for years, I mean we all were really. But he'd not been so bad when I last saw him, and that had been less than a month ago. I think hope was killing him.

He'd seen Inez, one of us, get clean and he wanted that. He didn't want to be tired any more. But she was gone, and no miracles were forthcoming for him, no matter how bad he wanted it. Someone out there had given him a sliver of hope, a chance at a new life, but had snatched it right away. And I was pretty sure it would kill him.

There was nothing I could do to fix that. I was no miracle worker. If I was, I wouldn't be living in a storage unit in Elk Grove, that's for fucking sure. I had no hope to give, to spare, to conjure. And I always made damn sure that any such tripe didn't linger around me too long. Shit wasn't healthy.

I tried to imagine what Inez must have felt. What it would be like to not ride herd on the demons in your soul with the demons on your back. To pull that ache, that itch, right out, sweat it from your pores and be done with it once and for all. I couldn't even fathom it. I'd been down so long that I'd forgotten what up felt like.

All these thoughts, it made one thing clear: Inez was dead. I wasn't sure where she was, or who had done it, but I'd decided there was no way you get shuck of all this and you don't go back to your kids. And if I had to lay money on it, my guess was that Hatty had something to do with it. Why he'd want to kill some old strung out woman I couldn't even begin to fathom.

But he'd lied to me, when he had no call to. Which as a preacher doesn't look too good. So it meant he did have a reason to lie to me, and no reason I could come up with put him in a good light.

I could call the cops I supposed, but I knew they would no more believe me than I would them. They had about as much faith in Inez as they would in anyone else they'd arrested a dozen times over the years, and would proceed to just write it off as her being on a bender somewhere. And if something wasn't done pretty quick, then the Reverend would be riding off into the sunset. I suspected tracking down itinerant preachers wasn't real high on anyone's list, so good luck then.

Finding who killed Inez wouldn't help Jerm either. He was gone in a way past helping, short of a miracle that would never come. But it would square things up at least a little. Because whoever killed Inez, they had basically signed Jerm's death warrant the same time.

And they might be fuckups, one and all, but goddamn it they were my people. No one else was looking out for us, with good reason I supposed, but some things you just can't let stand. Even as I thought it, I started cursing myself right the fuck out.

I kept cussing, and mentally beating myself up as I slipped the car into drive and turned back towards the Revival. I'd have to find some gas first though, because the Pontiac was about running on fumes.

Some gas, a pack of smokes, and a bite to eat. There went my fucking money.

Goddamn a good Samaritan.

19. Memory

I parked the Pontiac a ways down the road, cut up in a drive to a house so old and so far gone that it was little more than a pile of wooden slats. It was far enough up that it would be out of sight from anyone that wasn't looking real hard, and it was not like this road got a lot of traffic anyway.

I'd spent all my money on gas, pork rinds, a pack of smokes, and a Natty Daddy. I sat there in the car enjoying my bounty, making the most of it. Who knew, I might not be coming back. I might run into what did for Inez. And then wouldn't I feel the fool leaving behind a bit of meth and half a bag of pork rinds? Can't take it with you.

There wasn't any sort of plan in my head beyond 'wander up around the revival and scope things out.' It was about as terrible as most of my plans, but who was I to buck tradition this late in the game. I'd put more thought into what flavor of pork rinds to buy than that.

But with the tangy taste of bbq pork skin filling my mouth, I mused that sometimes it didn't take a lot of thought to nail it.

I was beginning to hum right along, my brain sparking in its usual terrible way. The Natty Daddy did next to nothing to even me out, but then it would take a lot more beer than one 25 oz to do that. That wasn't the intent though, not really. I just wanted a little liquid punch to the head.

Getting out of the car I left everything behind. I had nothing worth carrying. An empty wallet? If I died I wanted to make it as difficult for the cops as possible to ID me. One last fuck you. My cell phone? Dead as shit, and out of minutes. Keys? Who cared if I got locked out, or the car got stolen. Wasn't mine.

It was just me. Once more into the breech and all that bullshit.

I stood there, staring at the ruins of the house. I swear there are more abandoned, ruined buildings in Jubal County than not. No one ever took the time to clean them away, or at least burn them down. It felt like as a collective we just couldn't let shit go.

A wad of phlegm launched from my mouth as I spat on the closest slat. I missed, not that it mattered. If I was much of one for omens, I might have taken that poorly. Instead I just set off through the brush that surrounded me, making my way in a roundabout fashion to the pasture the revival was set up in. My guess was that it was about a mile away, maybe a touch more, but when you haven't owned a car in years, walking turns out to be no big thing.

At least that's what I thought til I got my first mosquito bite.

The best magic the world could have ever created was some sorta spell to keep the little buggers off you. But if it existed, I sure as hell didn't know it. At least by keeping a steady pace I limited how much they could get to me, but even still I got a few of the little bastards on me, and in the dark I never realized it till it was too late.

But at least it wasn't deer flies. That would have been even more of a bitch. Those pricks could snag you at a run if they had a mind to, and I'd certainly seen enough of them over the course of the day. They were bad this year, worse than I'd seen in a long time.

The woods were still wet with the passing storm, and water dripped from limbs above me. Every so often the breeze would blow hard enough to shake the trees a bit, sending a cascade of drops to shower on my head. It didn't much matter, seeing as my pants were pretty quickly soaked from brushing against wet brush. Why shouldn't my shirt match?

The moon was providing a decent amount of light, enough for me to be able to see fairly well. Enough that I didn't trip over every little log and hole in the forest. I could have called up a little light, but I was trying to be as discreet as possible, and the drugs coursing through me, they were damn near screaming, begging to fuel a bit of witchery. My impulse control has never been the best, so it was a struggle to not give in.

A sound began to reach my ears, and after pausing to hear better, I realized it was running water. There was a stream nearby it sounded like, off to my right. I veered off towards it, thinking it would be easier to walk along a creek bed than through thick brush.

It was a surprisingly large stream, several feet deep from the looks of it, and maybe twenty feet wide. It had cut pretty deep into the earth, and from where I stood, it flowed past perhaps six feet below me. I didn't feel like climbing down there, so instead I just walked along the top of the bank. It wasn't much improvement, but at least it spiced up the scenery a bit.

After a time I came to a barbed wire fence, the dividing line between the pasture land and the forest. I stood there in the shadows for some time, just staring out, looking for movement. The expanse of grass was silver blue in the moonlight, and it spread out over a low hilltop. I knew that the revival would be just on the other side of the hill, which was perfect. I could get over there unseen most likely.

Carefully I spread two of the strands of wire and contorted my way through, managing to not get my shirt caught on the barbs, or more importantly, my flesh. As rusted and old as the wire was, I'd have lockjaw before the week was out I'd bet if I had. But there is an art to getting past such fences, one I had honed over years of going into places I wasn't supposed to.

I kept walking along the stream. I figured if I ended up seeing lights, or someone coming, I could just jump down into the water and hide. That would get me most of the way there, then it would be just a short jaunt over the hilltop.

I'd made it almost as far as I had planned when the little bank I was walking along began to dip down. The stream was still about as deep, but it looked like this might be where the cattle crossed. Mr. Andrew had moved the cows to another pasture for the duration, but the lack of grass showed that many a hoof had trod here within recent memory.

A glimmer of a thought came to mind. All revivals like this did baptisms. Glancing up and down the silver thread of the stream, I could see that this was the only part easy enough to get down through to the water. And it was pretty clear someone had taken some time and a shovel to get rid of all the dried cow shit. My guess was this was where they did it, old school style.

Had Hatty said she'd been baptized? My memory said he did, I was pretty sure.

Closing my eyes a moment, I fixed the day and rough time in my mind. Opening them, I glanced up at the moon, and began mouthing a few quiet words. I did a little fiddling with my hands, but the real casting went on in my soul, as I pulled on the power inside me.

The moon holds memories, if you know how to call them up.

A faint shimmering glow covered the ground around me, spreading out towards the water. I focused on what I thought might be there, trying to picture it in my mind. A spell like this works much better if you saw it happen yourself, or know exactly what happened. But with enough power you could call up...

Spectral forms emerged from the glow, faint wisps at first that grew steadily more substantial with every passing moment. At first all you could tell was that there were two figures, but it soon became clear that one was Hatty, and the other Inez. She was leaning against him as they stepped into the water.

Their passing left no ripples in the stream, no real ones at least, as I watched Hatty dunk her under the water, having to bend low to submerge her. It wasn't until I saw her arms rise up out of the water that I realized how long she'd been under. I saw her start to fight, and the Reverend push harder, keeping her under.

I closed my eyes, not wanting to watch this anymore.

20. Red Lights Flashing

While I had my eyes closed, I cut off the flow of power. I knew what I needed to know now, unfortunately. When I opened them there was only the faintest hint of the spell left as it faded away to nothingness.

It was one thing to 'know' something bad had happened, and another thing entirely to actually know it. Inez was gone, and I'd been hired by an orphan to find her and bring her back. Talk about tilting at windmills. The only plus side to all this was I knew who killed her. Now I just had to decide what to do about it.

The cops wouldn't listen to me, but they might listen to an anonymous tip to the crimestopper line. That I could make happen. Maybe call and say I'd seen Hatty drown her. Maybe that would get the cops out here, and maybe they would find some sort of proof. Maybe he'd left some fingerprint or something on her car. I could drop that hint as well.

It was something. And I could tell her daddy. He probably wouldn't want to believe me, but he was that sort of protective, dogged sort of old man that wouldn't let it rest until some sort of answer was found. He also knew of Granny well enough to give what I say a little more credence than the cops.

Do that, and I'd be done with this. I didn't know where the body was, but maybe he'd just sunk her down in the stream. Or buried her nearby. They could get a dog out here to figure that out. Those cadaver dogs were something else I'd heard.

Thinking through all this helped distract me from thinking about my dead friend. Even if we hadn't been all that close, she meant a lot to Jimmy. And we'd spent a good bit of time together over the years, all things considered. Poor Thomas.

I'd make my calls when I dropped off the car I decided. I'd just pop up to the top of the hill, make sure Hatty was still there, and then dip out. I'd like to go down there and kill that son of a bitch, but I'd never killed someone before, and no matter how mad I got, I wasn't aiming to change that.

I was just below the line of the hilltop when I heard a door shut nearby. It was mighty late for Hatty to still be up I thought, so I quickly scuttled up the rest of the way up the hill, ducking down real low so I couldn't be seen, at least I hoped. Raising my head slightly, I looked down the hill towards the RV and revival tent.

The large tent was dark, the generator that ran the strings of lights having long been cut off. The camper was in clear view, its pale sides glowing faintly in the moonlight. For the first time I saw the small yellow Datsun truck that was parked alongside it. From the tent earlier it hadn't been visible, the sight of it blocked by the larger RV.

A pale square of light was shining from the window of the camper. Hatty stood there in it, a rifle in his hand. He was working the bolt on it, clearly checking to see if it was loaded. It wracked shut with an ominous snick, and he shoved a small box into his back pocket. More rounds I assumed.

Purposefully he strode over to the truck, carefully slinging the rifle into the passenger seat. He paused a moment before climbing in himself, his head bowed. My guess was he was praying, though if he said anything he was way too far away for me to hear it and it was too dark to see if his lips were moving.

My mind was racing. You see a murderer go climbing in a truck with a rifle this late at night, it's pretty clear he's up to no good. And the kind of no good you get up to with a loaded rifle, well that usually ended up with someone dead. What the fuck was he on about?

I thought back to our conversation. Had I done something to trigger him? Was it something I said? Had that spell or whatever set him off? I thought back, hard. If it was me he was after, well, that was of no matter. I wasn't where you would go looking for me. If he had some sorta spell hunting me, well, it would have told him I was right around and he wouldn't be getting into his truck.

He'd been surprised that Inez had more kids though. And it wouldn't take but a look in the phonebook, or a quick call or two to his congregation to find out just where Inez had been living.

I swore, and as he got into his vehicle, I turned and cut back down the hill. I broke into a run, and within seconds my smoke weakened lungs were protesting. Cursing and wailing more precisely, begging me to stop. I couldn't though. The thought that maybe I'd turned some psycho onto those kids had me right terrified.

The barbed wire caught my shirt, and raked a line across my back as I tried hurrying through the fence. I didn't care, just tugged my shirt free and took off through the woods. Limbs and brush tore at me, cutting up my arms a little, but I got lucky there, and managed to dodge the worst of it. I had to slow some, my lungs simply not having it anymore.

By the time I reached the Pontiac I was wheezing up a storm, and there was more staggering than running. I hit the side of the car, damn near collapsing, as I fumbled at the door handle. I was suddenly glad I hadn't bothered to lock it, because I was pretty sure my shaking hands would never have gotten the key into the lock.

I was ashamed of how out of shape I'd let myself get, but decided that just then was not the time for self-flagellation. At least not on that subject. Tomorrow, I would either take the time then, or be too busy beating myself up for causing a bunch of kids to die.

Of course that assumed I would be alive as well.

I really hoped I was overreacting. That ol' Hatty was just dipping out to go raccoon hunting, or to pop off a few possums or some shit. Maybe that was how he survived, munching wood rats to tide him over until the next big collection plate pull.

My gut was telling me I was wrong though. On the plus side, I was so focused on catching my breath again that the rocking of the shockless car didn't bother me half as bad. By the time I got the damn thing back on the paved road I could almost breath again.

I got the car going about as fast as I could, at least as fast as I felt marginally safe going. The old car didn't exactly have a lot of gumption, so racing along was not really in its wheelhouse. I got it up to around seventy on the straightaways, and that was about all it seemed it was willing to do.

Hatty would have a good head start, I knew that. I just had to hope that he would be going slower so as to not draw attention, and not being local he would have to find the place. But with my piss poor showing as a distance sprinter, hell, for all I knew he'd already gotten there.

I kept checking the rearview, expecting flashing lights at any second, but for once my luck held. There wouldn't be any talking my way out of this one if a sheriff stopped me, I knew that. And any sort of delay, well I reckoned that would be all she wrote.

I was coming up on Jerms, and I debated taking a second to try and roust him out as some added muscle. Or at least to maybe call the cops, get them moving. They wouldn't likely listen to me, but they'd probably listen to Jerm's momma. But could I spare the time?

As I whipped past going about sixty-five through the turn, passing Jerm's place, I still hadn't decided. I guess by not bothering to even slow I'd sorta made my choice, but it hadn't been all that conscious of a thought. It just sorta happened before I could decide otherwise.

Well, I was fucking committed now. It was me versus Hatty.

Assuming of course my drug addled paranoia hadn't just gotten me all whipped up into a frenzy for nothing.

21. Time To Retire

I hit the little dirt road the Richmond family called home going a good fifty miles an hour. I was lucky the Pontiac was so heavy, it kept the car from sliding all over the place as I veered from the paved road. It also served to make me hit my head against the roof, causing me to yell out in pain. It stung, bad, making my eyes water.

For a moment I prayed that would be the last time I had cause to curse the busted shocks of the car. Then I thought about that ominous-like, and decided I would happily bitch about them tomorrow if I was still alive. A sore head and even more sore ass was preferable to not being sore at all...ever again. In a casket.

It had been dark out on the main road, but here on a Jubal County backroad my headlights didn't so much cut through the darkness as get swallowed up by it. The cock-eyed lights weren't the best to begin with, and with the closely growing trees the moonlight had been choked off before it could reach through to light my way.

Two eyes reflected back at me, small and low to the ground. They started away from the car and for a brief moment I saw a possum go scuttling through the ditch, back into the woods. He was lucky he was smart, because I hadn't the time to slow down for anything smaller than a deer.

I passed the well-kept elder Richmond homestead. One lone security light lit up the back corner of the yard, but my quick glance showed there weren't any signs of life from inside the house. Early to bed, early to rise no doubt. I'd had a slight hope that maybe they were up doing something with the chickens, because sometimes the farms around here would get their deliveries of hatchlings at night. I hadn't a clue if Elias was one of them, but judging from the lack of lights shining back in the woods, I guessed even if he was, tonight was not his night.

Racing around the curve that led to the home I had left a lifetime ago that morning, my heart leapt into my throat. I didn't see the little Datsun anywhere. I cut loose a little whoop and eased my foot off the gas till I was going an actual reasonable speed.

I eased the car into the yard, directing its nose towards the barn. My eyes looked around, and sure enough, no truck, no Hatty. There was one light on in the trailer, but other than that, it looked like there wasn't much activity going on. So I parked the car and slowly got out, rubbing my aching backside.

There in the mouth of the barn I stopped, pausing to light a cigarette. The hand holding my lighter was shaking a bit I was surprised to find, and I took a moment to steady it. It did, after a minute or two and I tucked the Bic away in my pocket once more. I stood there in the shadows, the cherry of my cig a tiny red counterpoint to the light dusting of stars in the night sky above.

I heard a screen door shut, and my eyes darted to the trailer. Forrest had stepped out onto the little porch. "That you Marsh?" He called out in a low voice.

"Yeah, just me," I said. I held my ground. I was afraid I might look pale, scared. I didn't want him to see me like that, at least not clearly. It was better that I was in the dark.

He came padding across the yard barefoot, wearing a pair of grey sweatpants and an Auburn shirt a size too small. "I was beginning to think you'd done took the car and run off."

I snorted, faking a bravado I wasn't feeling. "Well I 'preciate you not calling the cops on me. Last thing I need is to be dealing with that shit."

"Eh, I knew better," he said. "Besides, I was too busy today, what with getting pipe run, and getting some damn seeds in the ground. Bout the time I got done with that, it was time to get everyone fed and in bed. And you can imagine how that went."

I could. Younger siblings never liked to listen to their older siblings, even when there was a parent around to enforce things. With Inez having been gone for so long...

"I didn't find her," I sighed. "I looked all over, all the usual spots, but..."

There was no way I was gonna be the one to break it to him that his mom was dead. I would do a crimestopper tip to get that ball rolling, but breaking that sorta news to someone? Shit, no fucking way, not if I could help it. Besides, it wouldn't make any real difference, not in the long run. I tell him what happened, and that just leads to questions that no cop will ever believe the answers to, and then boom, I'm on trial for murder.

Upstanding revival preacher, or druggie homeless degen. I know who the fuck their first suspect would be, if I tried coming at them direct with something like this. To. Hell. With. That.

I'll say though, it couldn't have turned out much worse than the look that boy gave me. The moral of the fucking night had quickly become 'hope is fucking poison.' The little bit of life in his face faded away, drained until his face matched the color of the moonlight.

"Em, I figured you wouldn't," he said bravely. "No worries." He sighed, then looked up at the night sky. I looked away, so as to not notice how much he was blinking. "I appreciate you taking the time to look. You spent all damn day on it, and it means a lot. I just wish I had some more money to give you."

I was about to say something, but my mind wiped itself right blank, right quick. There were headlights coming up the road.

22. So We Turned That Liquor Store Into A Structure Fire

"Uh, maybe I could..." the youth was saying. I cut him off.

"Hey, maybe we should take this inside. It's sort of dark out here and all. And I could use a drink if you got one to spare real quick." I was praying the headlights meant nothing. Just some teens out joyriding the backroads, or someone coming home from second shift at the Hyundai plant. But just in case...

"Yeah, I can handle that," Forrest said, making his way towards the house. "Sweet tea alright?"

"Sounds perfect. Lemme finish this cig, and I'll be right there." It wasn't until I went to take a pull on the smoke that I realized I had clenched my fingers so hard I had smashed the filter tight. *Tighten up Marsh.*

Forrest was almost to the little porch when the headlights came fully into view. The headlights attached to a small Datsun pickup truck that was cruising very slowly down the road. I could see the faint glow of a cell phone inside, as of someone looking at a GPS screen maybe.

The youth turned back to look at me. The trailer was between him and the truck, so he couldn't see it, but he must have heard it. "Someone pulling up?"

"Boy, get inside right now and hide. Hide your brother and sister too."

Forrest took a step towards me. "What?" He asked, confusion filling his face.

"Something bad is about to happen," I snapped. "Now git! Hide, and if you can, call the cops." He still stood there, taken aback. "Run boy!"

At last he took off, a few slow steps at first, then he broke into a sprint, skipping the steps and jumping straight up onto the porch. I didn't watch anymore however. I flicked my cigarette into the grass and started out of the barn.

The truck had passed out of sight for me as well, having moved in front of the trailer. But a sudden brighter red glow let me know that Hatty, it had to be Hatty, was hitting the brakes. I could still hear the engine as well, and I heard as it came to a stop.

I broke into a trot myself, needing to confirm who it was before I did anything rash. I wondered if I should have told the boy to take his family out the back, into the woods, but that ship had sailed. Crossing my fingers, I peeked around the trailer. It was definitely the preacher's truck.

I leaned against the corner of the trailer as the man got out of his vehicle, trying to look nonchalant. He'd parked the truck at the edge of the yard, pulled just off the road onto the grass. The engine still ran, but the reverend had killed the lights. He had the rifle in his hands. "What say you just get back in that truck and drive on," I called out.

Hatty froze, his eyes locked on me. I could see him gripping the rifle tightly in his hands, but as yet he didn't raise it up. Which was good, seeing as I had no weapon whatsoever. I shoulda taken more drugs, but I wasn't thinking my most clear. I'd already started calling up the power, but there was only so much I could do.

"I know what you done to Inez. I sent it, heard it from the moon, your little baptism. And I got to say, fuck you and everything about you. And I know it was my fuckup that you even heard about these kids here, so I'll be damned if I let anything happen to them." I rolled my neck hoping it would pop ominously, but no dice. I did stand up from my practiced lean and straightened my shoulders.

"You'll be damned anyway, witch," the man said. His voice wasn't angry, it was calculating. "I knew I smelled the stench of sin on you, and I'm actually glad you're here. Now I can cleanse this bloodline of its wickedness, and purge one more Satan-loving witch from the world at the same time."

"That was you that cast the spell back in the tent. I figured. Ain't that just delightfully hypocritical of you reverend." I tried to hang as much sarcasm on his title as I could. "Well I guess they do say it takes a thief to catch a thief."

An indignant look came on his face then, the first real emotion I'd seen. "My powers are a gift from the lord God on High, given unto me that I might fulfill biblical law. Exodus 22:18 'Thou shalt not suffer a witch to live.'"

"Well Marsh 4:20 says you can fuck right off." I spat in his direction. Had Forrest gotten him and the kids hidden yet? Had he called the cops? Was he doing something stupid even then like looking out the window to see what was going on?

"Smart words will not save you from your fate," he said, shaking his head. "If you repent, and beg forgiveness for your sins, then when I kill you, you may have some small chance at an entry into the God's blessed light. I will give you a moment to pray, sinner."

"Some sins boss, you just don't get forgiven," I said. I called up my power, and my hand became wreathed in blue-black flames. "You get gone, and you'll have plenty of time to pray for your sins in prison. Out of kindness, I'll give you the same chance you gave me, if you get in your car and drive the fuck off right now."

A snarl came upon his face then, real anger. He raised his hand from the barrel of the rifle, holding it up to match mine. With a word, his hand too erupted into a golden white fire, so bright it was like a tiny sliver of the sun come to earth.

"Now it's a party," I grinned ferally.

23.   Fist Full Of (Flaming) Dollars

I think I moved first, but if I did, it was only by a split fucking second. Practically as one we both hurled our flame covered fists outwards, hurling a ball of magical energy at each other with as much force as we could muster.

The two flaming orbs struck just over halfway between us, colliding a few feet away from a cement birdbath that was filled with water so stagnant it was damn near black. The heat of the flames instantly vaporized the water in a hiss of steam.

That was just the sideshow though. The real fireworks were happening a foot or so away.

My blue-black fire had struck the slightly larger ball of white-gold that Hatty had hurled. They hit with a crack like a gunshot, loud enough to hurt my ears. You could instantly smell an acrid singed odor, like burning insulation, enough to cause my eyes to water.

That wasn't helped by the explosion of colors that erupted before our eyes. The two fires entwined, black-gold and blue-white spiraling outwards like the birth of a hurricane. A crackling roar accompanied it as the flames chased each other in a riot of light.

I could see though that the Reverend's flames were the ones doing the chasing. The spreading nova of color was quickly becoming much lighter in its shading as tendrils of black were scorched from existence. A rain of ash was falling onto the blackened grass beneath, a circle of charred earth damn near scoured to the dirt.

This was just the matter of a few seconds, but I could see exactly how this was going to go. I was already shifting myself as the last few licks of blue were devoured. My turning head saw Hatty's creation hurling towards me, nothing stopping it now.

I tucked my head and dove behind the corner of the trailer. I stuck my arms out to try and catch my fall, but I was moving so quickly that I could do little more than just roll with it. My torso slammed into the rain dampened ground, knocking the breath from me.

Above, and slightly behind, I heard a crash and felt the heat of the orb singe the hair off my legs. I was pretty sure I was gonna have something like a sunburn there, but who had time to worry about a little burn just then. Lungs begging, I stumbled to my feet and took off.

Glancing back I could see that the corner of the trailer was on fire. The force of the strike had actually holed the metal slightly, ripping a tear in the tin exterior and catching the wooden skeleton of the frame alight. The magic had already faded, but the flames it left behind were all too real. I swore, hoping that wherever the kids were hiding it hadn't been in that room.

I heard Hatty shout something, but damned if I understood what he said. Probably some looney religious shit. I was too busy trying to catch my breath and stay alive to focus on his crazy, not if I wanted to keep staying alive.

With magic, I know that any folk who can actually do it are stronger than me. Most of them by a good bit. I don't know if it's cause of how they was trained, or if it's some sort of inside thing. Most folks with the power, they keep what they know all mighty close to the vest and don't go around sharing their secrets.

What I had learned to do to compensate was heavy drugs. I mean, I'd have done them anyway, let's be honest here. In fact I was using them recreationally long before I ever figured out how to tap them for more useful reasons. But they were how I bridged the gap in power.

Only, I usually had more in my system when shit like this went down. I'd been broke too long to be able to splurge like I normally would, and I was paying for it now. There was a lingering cocktail of substance threading its way through my bloodstream, but nowhere near as much as I would have liked.

But even if Hatty was now as tapped out as I was, which I really doubted, he still had a gun, and I had fuck all. I scrambled around the trailer, looking for anything that could help me. I was too far from the barn or tree line, and he would spot me before I could reach their momentary safety. There was a very slight chance I could dash inside the house, but it was a long shot, and that would just probably drag him right in after me, which was the exact opposite of what I wanted.

Then I saw it, and that sort of super cliche plan that you get from watching too many movies came. It was all I had.

The real kicker? It actually almost sorta worked.

24.   You Wanna Tussle?

Coming on at a run the Reverend came around the corner of the building hunting me. Now if it had been a movie, he'd have been right there next to the side of the trailer. But with that end of the place on fire, he had moved out a few feet.

So when I swung the shovel Forrest had been using to dig his trench that morning, instead of smacking the bastard in the face, it slapped into the barrel of the rifle. It hit with enough force to rip it out of the man's hands, sending it spinning backwards. It fired, probably from his finger getting snatched when I struck, but the bullet tore a harmless hole in the trailer skirting.

I swung for the fences, and in doing so, sorta overextended myself. My hands were ringing, jarred hard by the blow of metal on metal, and it caused my grip to loosen. I managed to keep grip with my right hand, but my left couldn't stick with it. So the shovel swung right around, past the point of easy control.

There was only a moment, and I knew spending it wrangling that shovel back into some sort of fighting stance would just leave me a scorched pile of ash on the grass. So I turned it loose. It hurled towards the trailer, and struck the side I think. I wasn't paying it much mind however, having squared up to do my best linebacker impersonation.

Football had never been my sport, but I bled Crimson, and had watched enough over the years to have the general idea down. Lunge forward, shoulder lowered, and try to wrap the bastard up. That was the plan.

What actually happened was that he turned slightly and managed to hammer a fist down on my back. I still struck him, and managed to get my arms around him, but instead of taking him to the ground, he just staggered back and tried beating my back into submission.

Those blows HURT. He had real strength, and one or two more and I would be pounded into the dirt. It was all I could do to keep my feet from the two smacks he'd already put on me, and I wasn't sure he hadn't cracked a rib.

But at the end of the day there was one difference between us: he was a preacher, and I was a degen. I'd lived in the gutter and fought like it. I was pretty small, both physically and in power, so I'd long ago learned to find ways to even the playing field. He wasn't ready.

I called up a bit of power and drove my fist right into his balls. Along with the force of the blow came a little bit of an electric shock courtesy of my magic. Sure, me touching him, it shocked me too a bit, but he got the worst of it. And in the worst possible place.

He crumpled to the ground with a shriek. I staggered back as well, my hair standing up on end from the current that had passed through me. But I managed to keep my feet, if only barely, and step towards him.

As he writhed there at my feet I knew how easy it would be for me to kill him. One fist full of flame, and he'd be a charred pile of bones in a few moments. He'd been trying to do the same to me and would, it seemed, happily do it to the kids inside.

He had killed my friend, and killed the hope of another.

I raised my fist high above my head. And then, more falling than anything, drove it down into his face. I felt his jaw crack under my hand, and felt bones in my own hand break as well. He went out, his writhing ceasing as I knocked him out.

Reeling back I clutched my hand to my chest. The pain was intense, and I was sure I had broken most of the bones around the knuckle of my pinky finger. I'll say this, it hurt like a mighty mother of a bitch, but it cleared my head right up from that electric induced grogginess. I was able to get to my feet easily enough. I thought about grabbing up that shovel and bashing Hatty's fucking face in.

Instead I looked over to the trailer. The corner of it was good and ablaze now, but so long as the kids weren't in that exact room, they would be fine, I figured. It would be no thing to get them out. As I looked though, I saw there were flames licking up over the roof from the front of the building.

25.   Fire It Up

The bastard must have slung another fireball at the front of the house. An insurance policy I guess. Swearing, I glanced back at him. He was down for the count, out like a light, whatever cliche you want to use. I'd have preferred to take the time to tie the bastard up, but I didn't have any rope.

I bolted for the back door, racing up the steps onto the gray, weathered boards of the back porch. Through the windows I could see an ominous orange light coming from what had to be the living room. I was reaching out my hand to open the door, when I heard a crash.

Off to my left a small window, barely six inches high shattered open. It was high up on the wall, and I knew the type; it was one of those little bathroom windows, designed to let in a little light, but be fairly creeper-proof at the same time. From behind it came screams.

Forrest I could hear clearly, shouting my name. But behind that was the screams of two other smaller voices. There was real terror there, and it fucking tore at me. "I'm coming!" I yelled. "Forrest I'm coming!"

I damn near ripped the screen door off its hinges, so hard did I yank on it. When I went to open the inner door though, I found that Forrest had locked it. I hardly slowed. Calling up on my rapidly diminishing well of power the door blasted off its hinges as a surge of pure force slammed into it. The heat hit me immediately I stepped into the hellscape.

The front of the house was ablaze in a rapidly expanding wall of flame. It was lashing out, spreading across the dingy carpet, and catching a couch alight. I shielded my face against it as I pulled my shirt up over my mouth and nose.

The heat was damn near unbearable, and I was across the room. The problem being, the hall that led to the bathroom was right there by the fire. If I got any closer, it really would be too much to handle. As it was, I was pretty damn sure my eyebrows were a little singed.

If I'd been properly dosed up, really humming along, I could have put that whole fire out more than likely. I can't do a whole lot of specific magic, but just generally controlling some of the elements, that I can do. Because that is less about training, and more about gut, at least so I have found.

But I was damn near tapped out, and my hand was all fucked up. I wasn't sure I could even really cast a good spell just then, with about half my fingers on that hand all buggered up. I felt a panic starting to well up in me.

Over the flames I could hear the kids screaming. That grounded me in a way that the fire right before my eyes couldn't. If I didn't move, they would die. I had brought this down on them. If they died, it would be all my fault.

I took off for the hallway. The heat started to blister my skin as I reached the portal, the orange flames reaching for me like grasping fingers. I called up the dregs of my power and did the best job I could at pushing away the heat. My fingers screamed as I twisted them to make the needed shape, but the heat abated just enough that I was able to make it past the worst of the fire.

Thick black smoke filled the air down to about my chest level, roiling out of the burning insulation. It made it so hard to see that I ended up ducking down, running as best I could bent over at the waist. Craning my head to one side I saw a doorway, but it was open and I could see what looked like a kids' bedroom with bunk beds. Cheap, dollar store toys littered the floor amongst the scattered remains of knock off barbies.

I should have known it would be the next door down. Every trailer, and damn near every house I have ever been in, the bathroom was the second door on the left. And, as usual, I was right. The door was shut, existing in a rapidly narrowing space across from two spreading fires looking to meet in the middle, right before that door.

Without slowing, I flung the door open. Sure enough, three huddled forms were curled up in the tub. Forrest had the shower going, and the water was falling on them, soaking them pretty solid. What smoke had bled in was being sucked out of the broken window. All in all the boy had done a good job, thinking of things it hadn't occurred to me to do.

All three looked at me, eyes wide with fright. The smoke, which had been seeping in before now came in rapidly, quickly filling the air. Luckily they were below the height of the smoke, being there in the tub, but I knew that wouldn't last long.

"Hush now, hush," I said, taking a knee beside the tub and putting my hands on the two littler ones. I looked at Forrest. "You did good, real good. It's time to go now though."

He shook his head. "We done tried. The fire's too hot."

I tried to smile as calmly as I could. I was the adult here, as sad as that was to say, and they were looking to me to be the stable one, the one with the plan. I had one - not great, but the best I could muster. I grabbed a handful of bath towels that were hanging on the racks, and shoved them in the shower. "Get these good and wet, and start wrapping them around you, especially your head."

The kids were too out of it, but Forrest started doing what I asked. While he did that, I stepped back to the doorway. That fire was moving, and moving quickly. Far quicker than it should have been. Whatever Hatty had done, a little bit of magic must have been lingering in the flames, making them far hungrier than they should have been. It sucked, but I planned to use it to my advantage if I could.

Just then the water died, sputtering to a stop. The water pipe must have burned through. As hot as this fire was burning, their clothes and towels would dry out damn quick if they got close to a flame. But it might buy a little time I hoped.

"Alright, c'mon now," I said helping the little boy from the tub. "We gotta be fast, but I bet you're real fast, aren't you?"

The kid nodded, but real unsure like. Forrest was up, hunched to keep under the smoke as much as possible, and was doing the same for his sister. Together we got them on their feet and up near the door. I looked at Forrest.

"You gotta trust me now, ok?" When he nodded I continued. "I'm gonna make it so you can stand the heat.

Don't ask, just trust. I need you to take their hands and run down the hall towards the corner over there. The fire done burned a hole big enough for you to jump through. Got it?"

He looked at me clearly unsure, but after a second he agreed. Then I dug deep, and told him to run. He ran, pulling those kids behind him like grounded kites.

I stepped into the hallway right behind him and snarled at my broken fingers til they contorted the way I wanted, forcing a narrow tunnel of power against the heat. It wasn't enough to really stop it, I didn't have the power for that, especially not over the length of the trailer that was left. But it was enough to keep their wet clothes from drying out too much, to keep them from catching fire. Tomorrow there would be blisters to doctor, and maybe missing eyebrows, but they would live. As long as they were quick.

Not surprisingly, Forrest was having some trouble guiding along his charges. I was too focused on maintaining the spell to even move, much less run along helping him, but as the strain of beating back the heat grew on me, I wished they would get it the fuck together. Keeping the heat off of them was doing little to keep it off me.

The little boy was going along, but it was clear he was scared, and not really on board with the whole happening. He kept stopping, having to be dragged along by his older brother. One time he fell and had to be picked up, but not before he got dragged again a few feet across singed carpet. That set him to wailing, and Forrest ended up just having to pick the child up. Luckily the little girl was going along more smoothly, or they'd never have made it.

Forrest set off running as best he could, pretty much dragging the girl behind him as the heat started to grow stronger. I could feel my spell weakening, and knew in a second or two it was gonna get reeeeal hot there around them. I could see steam rising up off their towels, and was sure it had to be filling their ears with a sizzling sound.

The hallway was narrow leading into the back bedroom, but I was able to see past the trio well enough that I could see a burning hole several feet wide, an orange glowing ring of fire. It was at this they were headed, as I watched the corner of the home start to sag and the supports burn out.

At the last second Forrest stopped, and with one fluid motion he flung his sister through the hole. She probably got a dislocated shoulder for it, and I heard her scream in fright and pain, but she was clear a half second later. With a shout Forrest followed, his brother held close to his chest. It was a near thing, the hole wasn't too tall, but the youth managed to duck low enough to not catch his head.

I damn near collapsed on the spot. Slumping into the doorway of the bathroom, I heard a crash as the end of the trailer fell in, the roof unable to support its own weight. A shower of sparks erupted, sending a torrent of flame and scorching heat down the hallway, right where I had been a moment ago.

26.   Hey There Hot Stuff

I was tapped, totally spent. I couldn't have summoned up a magic fart even if you'd filled me with ten bowls of magic beans. A hollowness, an aching empty, was all I had to offer just then. I felt like I had just lost a dozen pounds in sweat and sacrifice keeping that spell up long as I did, and it scooped out my insides more or less.

The smoke was getting worse, filling the air down almost to eye level as I sat there on the faux tile floor of the bathroom. My shirt had slipped down, so I pulled it back up over my mouth and nose, but even with that I started coughing. My eyes were watering up a storm as well, the smoke stinging them relentlessly.

I knew I needed to get moving, but I was also pretty sure there was nowhere for me to be moving too. Not really. There was no more water, no more towels, and I had no more magic to spend to keep the heat away. My only hope was to run towards the back door, but that would take me right through the fire, and I was pretty sure that was less than ideal.

Looking to the small, high window, I wondered if I could maybe pry it wider somehow. It was too skinny for me to crawl through now, but if I could get it a few inches wider, I could maybe squeeze through. It was hard to even see the window with all the thick black smoke, but my glance had me pretty sure that the frame was some kinda metal. And other than a grimy plunger there was nothing I could hope to even try to use to work at it.

As I looked, I heard a metallic thunk against the outside of the trailer, followed by a second then a third. It was a fairly small noise, but it was pretty clearly against the outside wall of the bathroom. I heard someone shouting my name too, Forrest, from the sounds of it. Then I got splashed in the face with water.

Someone had turned on the outside hose, the one I had helped get run that morning no doubt, and turning it on had gotten it through the window. It was way too small of a hose to do any good putting out the fire, but it would do just perfect for soaking me down.

I decided then that Forrest was a fucking genius, and wasted working in a damn chicken house.

Hose in hand, I began soaking my clothes as best I could while keeping below the smoke line. The water wasn't exactly cold, but it was a lot colder than all the heat around me, that was for sure. I didn't care, I just wished I had on long sleeves and jeans instead of shorts and t-shirt. I glanced at the shower curtain, but it was some sort of plastic, and the last thing I needed was a bunch of melted plastic covering me.

Thoroughly soaked, I wasted no time, and ran.

I ran blindly, through the smoke, not bothering to try and avoid it. There was no time. I was able to avoid the walls easily enough, because they were aflame, orange clear through the smoke. I could smell my hair burning, felt the scalding heat dry my clothes out, and steam rising from me. I had to jump over a burning end table. I almost tripped but managed, barely, to keep my feet and stop from falling into the roaring blaze that was the couch.

I hit the back door, ripping it open. The handle burned my hand, but I ignored it, leaping through onto the back porch. The corner of it had caught as well, but I was already jumping off it, slapping at my head and trying to put out the painful fire that was patches of my hair.

Someone tackled me, smothering me, and then I didn't know anything anymore.

27. Reunion

I was awake a good five minutes before I finally opened my eyes. Wherever I was, it was bright and well lit. I usually woke up in the darkness of my storage shed, or on the floor of Jimmy's camper, so I had to be someplace new. As vague memories began flowing through, the last thing I could remember was being on fire to some degree. And there was something wrapping my banged up hand pretty tightly. So I was likely in a hospital.

That is what finally got me to open my eyes. See just how bad a mess I was in.

Walls that had been real white maybe thirty years earlier surrounded me. Only now they were more of a dingy yellow and showing their years. A small tv sat on a little stand in the corner, on, but muted with the closed captioning running in its little black box at the bottom. Some sort of daytime talk show was on, but not one I recognized.

I groaned a little. Not because I was in any pain - because I really wasn't - beyond an assortment of aches. No, I was definitely in the Elk Grove Memorial Hospital, which meant medical bills. It would also mean real fast that I was going to be in a world of hurt if I didn't get out soon. Doctors tended to frown on meth use in their emergency ward I had found. I could already feel that itch crawling up my spine.

"So you're alive," came a familiar voice to my left.

I turned, and suddenly my heart skipped a beat. "H.D., didn't rightly expect to see you here. Though to be fair, I don't reckon I expected to see me here either."

My uncle smiled and nodded. "Well seeing as I'm listed as your emergency contact, figured I may as well sit around for a bit, make sure you were gonna be alright."

It got real silent there a second, that sorta awkward silence that probably only lasts like three seconds, but feels like an hour. I wasn't sure what to say, which while that would usually not stop me, I felt like things were too delicate for me to go running off at the mouth just then. H.D. was one of the only two friends I had, and as of late I had been beginning to think I might forever be down to just one. To see him here, now...

"Well," he started. "Don't nobody want to wake up all alone in a hospital. Even if they's mostly just faking being hurt." That last part was said with a wink and a broad grin.

Tension bled from that pregnant, silent moment, like a balloon being popped. I laughed a little, and held up my hand, which was wrapped in a bright pink cast. "Faking? Last I remember I was on fucking fire. And this cast ain't for show."

He grinned. "You can thank me for the color by the way. And on fire? Maybe just a little. You're gonna be walking around looking real surprised for a while, and you're missing more hair up top than you got, but the doc says it should grow back in just fine. Whole lot of fuss over nothing."

With my good hand I gingerly touched where my eyebrows had been, feeling the singed stubble that was left. I carried on up and a quick pat showed me he wasn't lying. It was real tender in a lot of places, and there was a whole lot of hair missing. "Well damn."

"I ain't heard the full story, what with being here with you, but so as you know the cops want to get your statement as soon as you're feeling up to it." He rose to his feet and stepped over to the open door, glancing up and down the hallway real quick. "I can read between the lines well enough though. You went down cause you overspent yourself, didn't you?"

I nodded. He was always harping on me that I should be trying to learn more about my powers and my limits, so I braced myself for a lecture.

"Overspent yourself on those kids, getting them out, not even worrying about yourself," he said softly. He looked at me, a warm look on his face. "I don't know if I've ever been more proud of you in my life, boy."

That caught me off guard, and I glanced down. I hadn't really been thinking about it in those terms, I'd just been doing what needed to be done. Especially as it had been my fault Hatty had even shown up.

I looked at my broken hand and sighed. "I guess since they called you, and already done this, it's too late to try and skip out on the bill? Blood suckers will find me and collect sooner or later."

H.D., clearly sensing I wanted to change the subject, smiled. "I wouldn't sweat it. Elias Richmond said he was gonna pay for everything. That it was the least he could do, all things considered."

He grew quiet a second. "There's a lot of questions swirling around, but at the end of the day, you saved them kids from the fire. That's what most folks will care about. Now, how about you tell me what actually happened, and we figure out the best way to spin this to the cops, so you don't get put into the nut house."

28. Don't Sweat It

H.D. was good enough to drive me home when they turned me loose later that day. Of course that ride home was real roundabout, with a good long layover at the County Sheriff's office. They kept me for fucking hours, but finally I was able to plead off with my cast and general hangdog look. They made it clear they had more questions, but were gonna cut me a little slack on account of how banged up I was.

Was I playing it up a bit? Maybe.

But also, they had some checking around to do first, to follow up on what my story was. They'd no idea about Inez, as I hadn't told Forrest about that. And while the boy had been able to clue them in on the fact that someone had attacked the place, and I had helped fight them off and get them out, he hadn't had a clue who it was.

Seems Hatty had gotten up and run off before the cops could show up. There was no doubt an APB or some such shit was out for him now, but I knew there was probably fuck all chance of them finding him in the short term. I had a suspicion this was far from his first time pulling some shit like this, and the fact that he hadn't been caught yet probably had no small amount to do with his magic.

I mean, if it could keep me out of prison, it could keep him out of jail, prison, or both, so long as he was smarter than me. Which looking at my life was a bit of a low bar I realized, but then what can you do.

Letting a bit of the small amount of drugs I had left flow into me, I leaned back in my broken recliner, thankful that the falling night had begun to cool things down a little for me. It made shed life almost bearable for a moment, and the drugs scratched that soul-deep ache in my spine.

All in all, I knew a whole lot of nothing about how everything was playing out. The kids were alive, and supposedly with their grandaddy. Word would get out pretty quick about Inez, especially if they found her body. There was no way I was gonna be the one to break the news to Jimmy. I mean, my cellphone was out of minutes anyway, so how would I let him know?

Same for Jerm, but I was mostly afraid of what he might do when he found out. I was worried about the little cuss, but there wasn't shit I could do about it.

I was no better off than I'd started yesterday morning. Looking at my hand, I realized I was actually worse off, though that was mitigated by the painkillers they'd sent me home with. A week's worth...they would get me through the rest of the night probably.

Silver lining of a sort.

Smoking my last cigarette, I sighed.

Fuck it, it'll all work out, or it won't, I decided.

Oblivion took me then, and that was that.

Acknowledgments

There are so many people to thank, that I am certain that I am going to forget some. To those people, you also have my apology!

Thanks to my family, who have always been supportive of my dreams, especially my parents who early on cultivated my love of books!

Thanks to Jon Marie, my LadyFriend, and the indomitable Riley, for being my biggest fans! You two make me feel loved and supported, and I hope I always do the same for you.

Thanks to my 'Crew,' both past and present: Amanda, Anthony, Baine, Cessaly, Chelsei, Chris, Derek, Derek (Other), Dusty, Elizabeth, Jenni, Joe, Kaye, Keith, Kristy, Lindsay, Rachel, Ryan, Shae, Tonya, Trey. Without you guys to help reign in this ego I don't know where I would be!

Thanks to my writing group, for helping hone my craft: Lacie, Brandon, and Les. Because sometimes Les is more. And a quick shout out to the RR Folks, you know who you are.

And finally I want to thank a few others who have supported me in all manner of ways: The Gump Plug Uglies, Dianne, Belles, Manda Mutiny, Stitch, Yukon, Jeff, and Beav.

About the Author

Born and raised in South Alabama, Bob has been writing as long as he can remember, though only began to take it seriously in the fall of 2012. That year he completed his first NaNoWriMo, writing a collection of short stories. This gave him the impetus to attempt to pursue a career as a writer. Since then, has written in a variety of genres: horror, southern gothic, steampunk, cyberpunk, and fantasy.

He has been published in several short story anthologies, has had several collections of his works published by Laser Blast Books, and has released a self-help book for creative people. Outside of that, he enjoys writing supplemental roleplaying material, is available to hire as a freelance writer, hosts a podcast, started a non-profit, occasionally delves into short film making, and loves puns in all forms.

Keep up with all his many projects at www.talesbybob.com or support him (and get sneak peaks and background material about the world of Jubal County) at www.patreon.com/talesbybob

You can hear his podcast, Books, Beards, Booze, wherever you get your podcasts. See more at www.booksbeardsbooze.com

The Music of Marsh

It is impossible to separate the music from the tale. Music has informed my every step, helping me set the mood as I forced this story onto paper. To see the complete Marsh Playlist you can check out my website.

For a short list of bands to check out though, start with the Builders and the Butchers. They are the largest influence, as if the title of these two novellas didn't tell you that already. But also check out: Tyler Childers, Lost Dog Street Band, Colter Wall, The Dead South, Horse Feathers, Possessed by Paul James, and All them Witches.

Printed in Great Britain
by Amazon

11056472R00166